Rostoff looked at Mathers and said, "Lieutenant, how would you like to capture a Kraden war-cruiser . . . single-handed? You would be certain to receive the Galactic Medal of Honor—and I'm sure you're aware of the privileges and opportunities that would then be yours."

Don laughed nervously, and replied, "I don't think there's any doubt that I'd be awarded the medal, Mr. Rostoff. But the odds against something like my One Man Scout capturing a cruiser are five hundred to one, at least. . . . it's not possible."

Rostoff leaned forward, his lupine face very serious. "Oh, but it is quite possible, my dear young lieutenant. In fact, my colleagues and I stand ready to arrange it for you . . . in return for certain considerations once you receive the Galactic Medal of Honor. . . ."

MACK REYNOLDS

GALACTIC MEDAL OF HONOR

WILDSIDE PRESS

GALACTIC MEDAL OF HONOR

Copyright © 1976 by Mack Reynolds

A much shorter version of this novel appeared in *Fantastic Magazine* under the title "Medal of Honor"

Unlimited power is apt to corrupt the minds of those who possess it.

—William Pitt, Earl of Chatham

Power tends to corrupt; absolute power corrupts absolutely.

—Lord Acton

I

After his craft had been mechanically wheeled away, Donal Mathers took one of the little hover-carts over to the squadron non-resident officers' quarters and showered, used a depilatory on his beard, then opened his locker and brought forth a dress uniform. He had thrown his coveralls into a disposal chute. He dressed carefully, checked himself out at the full length tri-di mirror, put his cap on his head, took a deep breath in unhappy anticipation, and headed for his fate.

The hovercart took him the kilometer or so to the administration buildings of the spaceport. He headed for the kingsize doors and the identity screen picked him up, checked him out in less than a second, and the doors opened before him.

Inside was bustle, the amount of bustle to be expected of a military establishment responsible for some two hundred spacecraft. Don Mathers was used to it. He made his way briskly to his destination.

A uniformed girl looked up from her work at the reception desk.

Don said, "Sub-lieutenant Donal Mathers, reporting to Commodore Bernklau."

She nodded and did the things receptionists do, and shortly looked up and said, "Go right in, Lieutenant."

He was about thirty years of age, slim of build and with a sort of aristocratic handsomeness in the British tradition. His hair was not quite blond, his eyes dark blue, his nose high and very slightly hooked. He affected a small moustache. He cut quite a nice figure in his light blue space pilot's uniform.

Now he snapped a crisp salute to his superior and said, "Sub-lieutenant Donal Mathers reporting from patrol, sir."

The commodore looked up at him, returned the salute in an off-hand manner and looked down into a screen set into the desk. He murmured, "Mathers. One Man Scout V-102. Sector A22-K223."

Commodore Walt Bernklau was a small man in the Space Service fashion. Overgrown men were no longer in vogue. Smaller men take up less room in a spaceship, breathe less air and require less food. It was not that a six-footer who weighed over 180 pounds was taboo in space but there was, perhaps, an unstated prejudice against him. Down through the centuries it had been the big man who received the attention, the small man who was a bit scorned. But those had been the days when war was waged with sword and battle-ax, and work performed by the

2

muscular. Things had been reversed. Even women, perhaps instinctively, had come to prefer smaller men.

The commodore wore the tired air of he who commands large numbers, of he who makes weighty decisions every day. He disliked the job but he was good at it. Pushing sixty, he looked forward to retirement.

He took in the younger man now and said, "You've been out only five days, Lieutenant."

Don Mathers said stiffly, "Yes, sir. On the third day I seemed to be developing trouble in my fuel injectors. I stuck it out for a couple of days but then decided that I'd better come in for a check." He paused only momentarily before adding, "As per instructions, sir."

The commodore nodded. "Ummm, of course. In a One Man Scout you can hardly make repairs in space. If you have any doubts at all about your craft, orders are to return to base. It happens to every pilot at one time or another."

"Yes, sir."

The commanding officer looked down into his screen again. "However, Lieutenant, it has happened to you four times out of your last six patrols."

Don Mathers said nothing. His face remained expressionless.

The commodore tilted his head slightly to one

3

side and said, "The mechanics report that they could find nothing wrong with your engines, Lieutenant."

The space pilot nodded agreement to that. "Yes, sir. Sometimes, sir, whatever is wrong fixes itself. Possibly a spot of bad fuel. It finally burns out and you're back on good fuel again. But by that time you're also back to the base."

The commodore said impatiently, "I don't need a lesson in the idiosyncracies of the One Man Scout, Lieutenant. I piloted one for nearly five years. I know their shortcomings—and those of their pilots."

"I don't understand, sir."

The commodore looked down at the ball of his thumb. "You're out in deep space for anywhere from two weeks to a month. All alone. You're looking for Kraden ships which practically never turn up."

"Yes, sir," Don said meaninglessly.

The commodore said, "We here at Command figure on you fellows getting a touch of space cafard once in a while and, ah, *imagining* something wrong in the engines, getting your wind up and coming in. But . . ." at this point the commodore cleared his throat, ". . . four times out of six? Are you sure you don't need a psych, Lieutenant?"

Don Mathers flushed. He said, "No, sir. I don't think that I do."

The other's voice went expressionless. "Very well, Lieutenant Mathers. You'll have the customary

4

three weeks leave before going out again. Dismissed."

Don saluted snappily, wheeled and marched from the office.

Outside, in the corridor, he muttered an obscenity under his breath. What in the hell did that chairborne brass hat know about space cafard? About the depthless blackness, the wretchedness of free fall, the claustrophobia, the tides of primitive terror that sometimes swept you when you realized that you were far away from the environment that had given you birth. That you were alone, alone, alone. A million, a seemingly million-million miles from your nearest fellow human. Space cafard, in a craft whose cabin was little larger than a good-sized closet! What did the commodore know about it?

Don Mathers had conveniently forgotten the other's claim to five years service in the One Man Scouts. And in the commodore's day the small spaceships had been tinier still and with less in the way of safety devices and such amenities as video-tape entertainment.

Still fuming with inner indignation, he recovered his hovercart and made his way from Space Command Headquarters, Third Division, to Harry's Nuevo Mexico Bar, which was located on the outskirts of the spaceport, just beyond the main entrance. It was a popular watering hole if only because it was the first one available when you left the base. In a way it was an anachronism since it had a live bartender. The trend, these days, was toward automation even in restaurants and bars. Live personnel in such establishments meant that their labor was not available for industry, for the all-out effort against the Kraden enemy. Harry, of course, was beyond retirement age and no pressure was put upon him to fold up his beloved establishment so that he could work elsewhere.

It was hardly conceivable to Don Mathers that anyone in his right mind would be so smitten by space that after a near lifetime of work as a second class mechanic, he would open a bar near the spaceport so that he could continue to associate with active spacemen and those who aided them. But that was Harry Amanroder.

Don dismissed the hovercart and it turned and headed back for the base motor pool. He entered the Nuevo Mexico and found it all but empty. There were a couple of mechanics in soiled coveralls over in a booth in the corner; both of them women, both of them drinking exotic-looking cocktails that made Don wince.

He climbed up onto a stool at the bar and beckoned to Harry, which was hardly necessary since the old-timer was already headed in his direction.

Harry Amanroder was somewhere in his mid-sixties, was heavy-set and big, which was possibly one of the reasons he had never been able to get into space, his life-long dream. His had been the fate to serve those who had attained his dream—and most of them, including Don Mathers, hating it. His pudding face shone when he served an active spaceman, his eyes lit up when he was able to lean on his bar and listen in on their conversation. He loved them all and most of them were tolerant of him.

He said now, "Cheers, Lootenant. What spins? Thought you was due for a patrol along in here. How come you're back so soon? Din't expect to see you for maybe another couple of weeks."

Don Mathers looked at him coldly. He said, "You prying into security subjects, Harry? I was on a . . . special mission. Top confidential."

Harry wiped the bar with a dirty bar rag, distressed. He said, earnestly, "Well, gee, no Lootenant. You know me. I know all the boys. I was just making conversation."

"Well, make it with somebody else," Don said with less than graciousness. "Look, Harry, how about some more credit? I don't have any pay coming up for a week. My Universal Credit Card is down to its last few pseudo-dollars."

"Why, sure, Lootenant. I ever turned you down? You're into me more than anybody ever comes in here. But, you know me. I never turned down a spaceman in my life. And that goes double for a real pilot. I got a boy serving on the *New Taos*, you know, the light cruiser."

Don Mathers knew, all right. He'd heard about it often enough.

Harry was saying, "Any spaceman's credit is good with me. What'll it be?"

"Tequila."

Tequila was the only concession the Nuevo Mexico Bar made to its name, save two sick cactus plants in pots which flanked the entry. Otherwise, the place looked like every other bar has looked in every land and in every era, save the new automated, sterile horrors that were taking over these days.

Harry turned and reached out for a bottle of Sauza. He put it on the bar and took up a lime and cut it into four quarters, then reached back and got a shaker of salt. He took a two-ounce shot glass and filled it carefully with the water-colored liquid H-Bomb.

Don went through the routine. He sprinkled some of the salt on the back of his hand, licked it, picked up the shot glass and tossed its contents back over his tonsils, then hurriedly grabbed up one of the quarters of lime and bit into it.

He said, "I'll be damned if I know why anybody punishes themselves by drinking this stuff."

Harry leaned on the bar before him and said, sympathetically, "You know, Lootenant, I don't either. I'm a beer-drinking man myself. But, you know, the kind of beer they're turning out these days, they could stick it back in the horse. No body, no strength, no nothing." He sighed. "I guess it's all necessary on account of the war effort. But we still had real beer, back when I was a kid."

"I doubt it. I remember my grandfather, back when I was a boy. He used to tell us, and over and over again, that the beer in those days wasn't worth drinking. No hops, no strength. Now when *he* was a young fellow they really had *beer*. I bet the complaint has gone back to the Babylonians, or whoever it was that first brewed beer."

Harry never argued with a real spaceman. He said, "I guess you're right, Lootenant. Like another one?"

"Yeah, hit me again," Don said. In actuality, in his humor, he wished he could think of something really cutting to say to the fawning bartender, but it was too damned much effort.

Harry poured more tequila.

He said, "You hear the news this morning?"

Don said, "No. I just got in. I've been in deep space."

He knocked back the second drink, going through the same procedure as before. He still didn't know why he drank this stuff, save that it was the quickest manner of getting an edge on.

"Colin Casey died." Harry shook his heavy head. "The only man in the system that held the Galactic Medal of Honor. Presidential proclamation. Everybody in the solar system is to hold five minutes of silence for him at two o'clock, Sol time."

"Oh?" Don said, in spite of his humor, impressed. "I hadn't heard about it as yet."

Harry said, "You know how many times that med-

al's been awarded since they first started it up, Lootenant?" Without waiting for an answer, Harry
added, "Just twelve times."

Don said dryly, "Eight of them posthumously,
and most of them as a result of the big shoot-out with
the Kradens."

"Yeah," Harry said, leaning on the bar again. His
other two customers didn't seem to require attention.

He added, in wonderment, "But just imagine.
The Galactic Medal of Honor, the bearer of which
by law can do no wrong. You come to some city,
walk into the biggest jewelry store in town, pick up
a diamond bracelet and walk out without paying.
And what happens?"

Don growled, "The jewelry store owner would
probably be over-reimbursed by popular subscrip-
tion. And probably the mayor of the town would
write you a letter thanking you for honoring his
fair city by deigning to notice one of the products
of its shops. Just like that."

"Yeah." Harry shook his head in continued awe.
"And, imagine, if you shoot somebody you don't
like, you couldn't spend even a single night in the
Nick."

Don said, "If you held the Galactic Medal of
Honor, you wouldn't have to shoot anybody. All
you'd have to do is drop the word that you mildly
didn't like him, and after a week or so of the treat-

ment he got from his fellow citizens, the poor bastard would probably commit suicide."

Harry sighed. "And suppose you went into one of them fancy whorehouses, like in Paris or Peking. Anything would be free. Anything."

Don snorted at the lack of imagination. "Why not just go out to New Hollywood? Look, Harry, mind if I use the phone?"

"Go right ahead, Lootenant. Anything you want in the place, until two o'clock. Then I close down for the rest of the day, on account of Colin Casey."

Don knew the Colin Casey story. Everybody knew the Colin Casey story. He had been a crewman on one of the Monitors, the heaviest of Solar System battle craft. When one of the reactors blew he had gone in immediately, improperly shielded, and had done what had to be done. His burns, though treated by the most competent physicians on Earth, had led to his present death, but he had saved the ship and had lived long enough to be awarded, though not to enjoy, the highest decoration the human race had conjured up. Yes, Don Mathers had known of Colin Casey—but hadn't envied the poor damn fool. Sure, they had kept him alive for years, but what good is life when you're blind, when you're sexually impotent, when you can't even walk? Precious little good the Galactic Medal of Honor had done Colin Casey.

He could have used his pocket transceiver to call

Dian Keramikou but the screen was so small that he wouldn't have been able to make out her features very well and even though he had seen her less than a week before, he wanted to feast his eyes on her.

In the phone booth he dialed and almost immediately the screen lit up and the face of the woman he loved faded in.

Dian Keramikou was a great deal of woman. Possibly five feet eight, possibly 134 pounds, possibly 39-25-39 and every inch glossy and firm. She wasn't truly a pretty woman. Her features were too vital and just slightly heavy. The brows were heavy, her hair harsh and black and glossy, like a racing mare. She had Indian-black eyes, a bold nose and a broad mouth. Not pretty, no, but strikingly handsome in the Greek tradition which she had inherited from her forebears.

She was obviously in the process of packing when the screen had summoned her. She looked into his face and said, in that slightly husky voice of hers, "Why, Don. I thought that you were on patrol."

He said, a little impatiently, "Yeah. Yeah, I was. However, something came up and I had to return to base."

She looked at him, a slight wrinkle on her broad, fine forehead. She said, "Again?"

He said impatiently, "Look, Di, I called you to ask for a get-together. You're leaving for that job on Callisto tomorrow. It's our last chance to be together.

Actually, there's something that I wanted to ask you about. Something in particular. It might change your mind about Callisto. I don't know why you're going, anyway. I've been there. It's a terrible place, Di. There's no atmosphere. You live under what amounts to a giant inverted plastic fishbowl."

"I've read up on Callisto," she said in irritation. "I know it's no paradise. But somebody has to do the work there and I'm a trained secretary. Don, I'm packing. I simply don't have the time to see you again. I thought that we said our goodbyes six days ago."

"This is important, Dian." His voice was urgent.

She tossed the two sweaters she was holding into a chair, or something, off-screen, and faced him, her hands on her hips.

"No it isn't, Don Mathers. Not to me, at least. We've been all over this. Why keep torturing yourself? You're not ready for marriage, Don. I don't want to hurt you, but you simply aren't. Look me up, Don—in a few years."

"Di! Just a couple of hours this afternoon." He was desperate.

Dian Keramikou looked him full in the face and said, "Colin Casey finally died of his burns and wounds this morning. The President has asked for five minutes of silence at two o'clock. Don, I plan to spend that time here alone in my apartment, possibly crying a few tears for a man who died for me and the rest of the human race under such extreme condi-

13

tions of gallantry that he was awarded the highest honor of which man has ever conceived. I wouldn't want to spend that five minutes while on a date with another member of my race's armed forces who had deserted his post of duty."

Don Mathers turned, after the screen had gone blank, and walked stiffly back to the bar. He got up on the stool again and called flatly to Harry, "Another tequila. A double tequila. And don't bother with that lime and salt routine."

II

By evening he was drenched, as the expression went these days. When Harry had closed the Nuevo Mexico at two o'clock, in memory of Colin Casey, Don Mathers had summoned a hovercab and dialed the hi-rise apartment house where he quartered himself in Center City.

He took one of the vacuum elevators up to the 45th floor and staggered to his mini-apartment. A mini-apartment was all he could afford on his sub-lieutenant's pay. In fact, he shouldn't have afforded that. He could have stayed considerably cheaper, living in bachelor's quarters on the base. But in the last year he had become so fed up with the Space Service that he preferred to stay away from any contact whenever he could. Besides, he'd had high hopes of Dian capitulating to him, with or without marriage, and wanted a place to be able to bring her.

She was a strange one, he had long since decided, when it came to sex matters. So far as he knew, she

15

was a virgin, in an age where it was no longer considered necessary or even very sensible to remain one after your mid-teens; though of recent date there had been somewhat of a swing of the pendulum in that regard, a newly swelling Victorianism, a return to the old virtues. Don Mathers supposed that it was a result of the Kraden threat and the possibility of human annihilation. The Universal Reformed Church was said to be growing in all but a geometric progression.

His identity screen picked him up, upon his approach, and the door automatically opened.

He entered the apartment and looked about distastefully. Wasn't it bad enough spending weeks at a time in a One Man Scout to have to return to quarters as small as this automated mini-apartment? Functional it might be, attractive it was not. A living room-cum-bedroom-cum study. A so-called kitchenette with small dining alcove; so-called because he never utilized it for more than making coffee. A small bath. Most of the furniture built in, very neatly, very efficiently.

He stripped off his uniform and hung it in the closet and brought forth civilian garb and redressed. The SPs, the Space Police, took a dim view of any spaceman, even an officer pilot, being seen in public intoxicated, and Don Mathers was already drenched and had every intention of getting more so. Everything and its cousin was going wrong. Dian was leaving tomorrow for the ridiculous job on the

Jupiter satellite, Callisto. He was on the commodore's S-list and most likely would be on it in capital letters shortly, because the fact of the matter was he was rapidly getting to the point where he couldn't bear the space patrols. Sooner or later, Bernklau was going to insist on a psych on him. Then the fat would really be in the fire, because under a psych they broke you down completely, entirely, and when they did that the medicos were going to find out that Don Mathers, for some time, had been planning on desertion.

In actuality, he would have gone over the hill long since had he been able to figure out some method of swinging it. In this day of International, actually Interplanetary, Data Banks, it wasn't the simplest thing in the world to try and disappear and take up a new identity. With Solar System wide unity, you couldn't run to some country where they wouldn't extradite you. And, for another thing, you simply couldn't survive without a Universal Credit Card. Money, as known in the past, was non-existent. Everything, but everything, was bought with your credit card. When you *made* some money, some pseudo-dollars, it was deposited to your account in the data banks. When you bought either an item or a service, the amount was deducted.

And for still another thing, every bit of information about you since your day of birth was in the data banks, on your Dossier Complete. Hell, before your birth. They also had complete rundowns on not only your parents, but—according to your age—usually your grandparents as well.

Of course, theoretically he could take off to some remote spot, and there were few enough left in the world, and live a hermit's life. He could become a present day Robinson Crusoe. Theoretically. But the life didn't seem a particularly attractive prospect.

However, he was checking out an alternative. There were some areas, for instance the Amazon basin in what was formerly called Brazil, which were now being developed in an all-out manner. It was said to be chaotic there. Everything fouled up. He was investigating the possibilities of getting down there and assuming a new identity. Possible? Maybe.

But now, immediately, he had three weeks before him to supposedly recuperate from his last patrol, even though he had spent only a fraction of it in space.

He could have done his additional drinking right here in his mini-apartment. His small autobar would have supplied him with all the ersatz guzzle he could dial. But he didn't want that. He didn't want to be completely alone after even only five days of patrol. He wanted people around, even though they didn't talk to him, associate with him. He just wanted them around. As a matter of fact, he didn't particularly want companionship, save that of Dian Keramikou, in his present state of mind. He wanted to suffer in silence.

He had lied to Harry Amanroder, in the Nuevo

Mexico. He wasn't particularly short financially. He had put his drinks on the cuff so that he could hold onto enough pseudo-dollar credit to show Dian a really big time. He had planned to take her to the Far-Out Room, located in the biggest hotel in Center City, and blow her to the finest spread possible. No whale steak, no synthetics. The real thing. From hors d'oeuvres to real fruit for dessert.

But now he planned to blow it on more guzzle.

And not in this building, either. There were several dozen bars, nightclubs and restaurants in the high-rise and he had, in his time, been in all of them. But not tonight. Tonight, he wanted to pub crawl, and preferably in the cheapest areas of town. Why, he didn't know, but he felt like slums, or the nearest thing to them the present world had to offer.

One automated bar faded into another. He seldom had more than one drink in any of them. He would sprawl at an empty table, put his Universal Credit Card in the payment slot and dial a tequila, or whatever. By this time he was mixing his drinks and feeling them to the point where he usually had to close one eye to be able to dial.

It was well into the night when the fog rolled out of his brain and he realized that he was zig-zagging down the street without remembering the last bar he had been in. He tried to concentrate. Had it been that one where the garish looking girl, or rather woman, had tried to pick him up? The place with the overly loud, harsh canned music and the overly loud, harsh crowd of drunks? He couldn't remember. He had blacked out, somewhere along the line. He was going to have to get to a metro station and take the vacuum tube back to his apartment house. If he passed out on the street and was thrown in the drunk Nick, they'd turn him over to the Space Police when they learned his identity and then he *would* be in trouble.

And suddenly he was confronted by three men in the uniforms of Space Platform privates. In the Space Service those who manned the heavily armed Space Platforms which orbited not only Earth but Luna, Mars and the colonized satellites as well, were the low men on the totem pole. Of all the elements in the service, theirs was the least glamorous, the most undesirable. In a way, the platforms were something like the Foreign Legion forts in the Sahara, a couple of centuries earlier. The space cafard incidence was high, particularly in view of the fact that a tour of duty lasted six months. Six months confined to a Space Platform! Most spacemen shuddered at the idea.

But now, here were three of them. And they stood there, blocking the way of Don Mathers. They averaged about his own build and they, too, were somewhat drenched, though not nearly as far gone as Don.

Two of them carried what appeared to be improvised truncheons, the other, the largest of them, had his fists balled.

"What the hell do you want?" Don slurred.

"Everything you've got, you funker," the largest one growled lowly. "Hand it over, or we take it the hard way—for you."

Don tried to rally himself. He said in a belligerent slur, "Look, you three, I'm a One Man Scout pilot, and officer. If you don't clear out, I'll summon the SP and it'll be your ass."

One of the others grinned nastily. "You reach for your transceiver, *sir,* and I'll bat you over the head with this."

Don Mathers wavered on his feet. Three of them, damn it, and he was drenched to the gills. He backed up against the wall of the building he had been walking along at their approach. He realized that if he'd had good sense he would do what they demanded. Precious little he had on him anyway, and most of it personal rather than being of much value; his transceiver, his class ring, his wrist chronometer, a gold stylo Dian had given him for his birthday a year ago when she still thought she was in love with him. It was the stylo that decided him; he didn't want to give it up.

He put up his hands in a drunken effort to defend himself.

It wasn't actually an age of personal physical violence. Don Mathers couldn't remember having hit anybody since childhood, and early childhood at that. Pugilism was no longer practiced as a sport, nor was wrestling, not to speak of judo or karate. Even football, basketball and hockey had been so modified as to minimize the danger of any of the contestants being hurt. Bullfighting and even auto racing were unknown. Men didn't kill each other, or get themselves killed in sports . . . when the Kradens were out there. Oh, he'd had some hand-to-hand combat while in cadet training, but not as it had been in the old days.

The three of them moved in on him carefully, and spaced out so that he couldn't face them all at once. They were going to be able to do whatever they wanted with him.

Suddenly, one reached out with his truncheon and whacked Don across the belly, hard.

Don's face went white. He brought his hands down over his guts and doubled forward. He vomited onto the sidewalk, the contents of his stomach burning acid and alcohol as it spewed out of his mouth. Even in his agony, his mind was clear enough to anticipate another blow of the club on his head momentarily. There was nothing that he could do about it.

But it was then that Thor Bjornsen exploded onto the scene. Where he came from none of the four participants in the drama ever comprehended. It was as though magically a giant had materialized in their midst. A berserk giant. And, in spite of his size, a veritable flurry of movement.

Don Mathers, still in agony, never did quite comprehend the next few minutes—if it lasted that long. Blows were struck and received, most of them going one way—from the giant out. In a moment, two men were down on the sidewalk, one sitting and looking startled, one sprawled flat.

And the next thing Don knew, the giant was chasing his three attackers down the street, one of the truncheons in hand and whacking them unmercifully on their buttocks as they went.

He returned shortly, chuckling. He cut off the laughter when he saw Don sitting on the curb and said, "Are you all right?"

"No," Don said. "I'm sick."

"You smell drenched."

"I am . . . or was."

The other peered down at him, quizzically. He said finally, "Well, whether or not, you're in no shape to be getting yourself home. My apartment's nearby. Come on over there. You can sleep on the couch. By morning, you should be able to hold down an Anti-Alc. I've got some. I too, in my time, have been drenched."

He helped Don to his feet, and, still holding him by one arm, led him along.

The big man said, "What did those three want?"

"They said they wanted everything I had."

Thor Bjornsen grunted. "You're fairly well dressed. They probably figured they could hock your things for enough pseudo-dollar credits to buy a few drinks. It's a queer world we're living in. For half a century we've been at peace, but preparing for war. We're in continual training for conflict that doesn't come. Violence is in the air and can't be sublimated with real violence against an enemy. So it sometimes comes out in some type of manufactured real violence, in short, masochism. Those three that jumped you didn't really need what little credits they would have realized. What they really wanted was the fun of working you over."

The other's apartment was in one of the older of Center City's buildings, rather than in one of the new hi-rises. And, being of an earlier era, the apartments were larger. Although a single, the place must have been twice the size of Don's mini-apartment. And it was considerably more comfortably furnished and decorated, for that matter.

His rescuer got Don into a chair and looked down at him, fists resting on his hips.

He said, "Can I get you anything?"

"No. I'll be all right in a minute or so." But Don doubted it.

"You don't think you could hold anything, any food, on your stomach?"

"Almighty Ultimate, no."

The other said, "My name's Thor Bjornsen."

Don looked up at him. "You look like Thor. I'm Sub-lieutenant Donal Mathers."

"Space Forces?"

"Pilot of a One Man Scout."

"Oh? I don't envy you that job."

Thor Bjornsen lived up to the first impression he had made on both Don and his attackers. He was a giant of a man in the Viking way. Red of hair, square of face, light blue of eye, graceful of carriage in spite of his brawn. Neither of them would have known, but physically he was a Norse version of the Joe Louis of an earlier time. In age he must have been roughly the same as Don Mathers, but his face had a boyish quality that made him seem more youthful.

He went over to an old-fashioned autobar set in the corner, rather than built-in, and dialed himself a drink, a stein of dark beer, and returned with it. He sat down on the couch across from Don's comfort chair.

He took a pull at the beer and said, "What in the hell were you out on the streets in this condition for?"

"I was drowning my sorrows," Don said ungraciously. "I should thank you for coming to the rescue. How could you possibly have taken on three men, two of them armed, and run them off?"

"Nobody knows how to fight any more," the other told him. "I make a hobby of it. I'd rather be able to knock down my enemies than drink my friends under the table. What sorrows?"

Don wondered if he felt like answering that. It was none of the big man's business. However, he said, "My girl left me to take a job on Callisto. And my commodore's down on me because I've had a series of troubles with my One Man Scout and have come in several times from patrol prematurely."

Thor Bjornsen finished his beer and stood again. "You look like hell," he said. "The bathroom's over there. I'll order some bedding from the ultra-market and we'll fix up that couch for you. You'll be better in the morning. Hell, by the looks of you you couldn't be worse."

In the morning, Don Mathers did feel worse, but in a different way. By the time he awoke, his host had already dressed.

He stood next to the couch, with a small bottle in his hand and shook a pill from it. "Anti-Alc," he said. "Here, take it down."

"It's against regulations for an officer of the damned Space Service to take the stuff," Don told him.

"Why?"

"I don't know. I think they want you to suffer. If you suffer enough from drinking, maybe you'll do less drinking, and they don't like pilots, in particular, to have their reflexes slowed up with guzzle."

Thor reached out the pill again, and a glass of water. "Tell them to get poked."

Don downed it, choking slightly, flushed it on through with the water. He began to feel better almost immediately, as he knew he would. He had taken the sober-up before, and many a time, in spite of what he had said about regulations.

26

The big man eyed him carefully and said, "You don't like the Space Service, do you?"

Don Mathers considered that for a minute before saying, "Well, no. But what can you do?"

"Get out. I did."

Don was surprised. "Were you in space?"

"I used to work on the radio interferometers on Luna. They're radio telescopes in which two or more antennas are connected to a single receiver. Our job was scanning space for signs of Kradens."

"I know what they are," Don growled. "How did you get out? That's a hell of a job, being stuck there in those underground towns on the moon."

"Medical discharge."

"There's nothing wrong with me, damn it."

Thor looked at him. "Would you think that there's anything wrong with me? I have a doctor friend. He can *make* something wrong with you, or seem to be. And he's available."

Don brushed it all off. He said, "I don't have any large lump sum of pseudo-dollars to pay out. All I have is my sub-lieutenant's pay."

"No charge."

Don contemplated him for a long, long moment. He was on delicate ground now, in view of his own thoughts about desertion. And he didn't really know this man. He said carefully, "You don't sound very patriotic, Thor. You forget the Kradens."

Thor Bjornsen shook his head. "No I don't. You can't forget something that doesn't exist."

27

Don fixed his eyes on him as though the other was demented. He said and his voice was angry, "That doesn't make any sense at all."

The other said, "I think it does. Keep quiet for a minute while we have some background." He thought about it for a minute before saying, "I'm not contending that the Kradens didn't once appear. Obviously, they did. Almost fifty years ago. Out of a clear sky—or, rather, out of clear space—they came. About twenty of their various sized and shaped spaceships. In spite of our radio telescopes trying to pick up intelligent broadcasts from space, and in spite of our own tight beam laser broadcasts sending out our own messages, the human race couldn't have been more surprised if we had one and all suddenly sprouted rhinoceros horns. We were floored—momentarily.

"At the time there were four spacepowers, if we can call them powers. They were pretty much in their infancy, so far as the military in space is concerned. They were the United States of the Americas, the Soviet Complex, Common Europe and China, in that order. The Asian Alliance and India also had embryonic space warcraft but they hardly counted at the time.

"In actuality, from the first man's explosion into space was basically a military and national prestige thing. We did a great deal of oratory about pure science and cooperation between the nations but even from the beginning spy satellites were sent up for military espionage purposes. Before long, first the United States and the Soviet Complex, and later the others, began to send up primitive military spacecraft armed with such weapons as could be designed for space combat at that time, largely missiles with nuclear warheads. Before very long, the early two or three man ships evolved into small cruisers with eight or so men aboard. Weapons became more sophisticated and we saw laser beam weapons, popularly called death rays, developed.

"We were at that stage, when the Kradens materialized. What they wanted we'll possibly never find out."

"We know what they wanted," Don protested.

Thor Bjornsen ignored him. "It was immediately assumed, the human mentality being the human mentality, that they had come to conquer Earth. Why they would want to the Almighty Ultimate only knows. Perhaps they were an exploring expedition; perhaps they were a colonizing expedition looking for new worlds, which doesn't mean, necessarily, that they would take over a suitable world by force, if it was already supporting an intelligent life form. It is to be assumed that if they had the technical ability to cross space, they would have a more sophisticated ethic than we possess. A culture does not progress technically without also progressing ethically. If it didn't, it would probably blow itself up, as we almost did on Earth shortly after the discovery of such super-weapons as nuclear bombs."

"Come on, come on," Don protested. "I don't need a lecture on ethics."

"Very well. Each of the four Earth powers with space fleets had patrols out at all times. Of a sudden, they were no longer four space fleets but one. And as a man they thundered in on the strangers from space. I would assume that it took the extraterrestrials by shock. Suddenly they were under attack, and under attack by the equivalent of the Japanese kamikaze fighters of the Second World War. Perhaps the Kradens attempted to defend themselves, but we aren't even sure of that. We don't really know if they were armed, and some strange tales and rumors have drifted down to us."

Don said indignantly, "Are you completely drivel-happy? They destroyed more than twenty of our spacecraft!"

The other looked at him thoughtfully. "I can't prove it, but I've often wondered whether our spacecraft didn't shoot each other down, or blow each other up, by mistake. Please remember that though they thought themselves fighting a common foe, they weren't coordinated. They entered the fight as four different space forces. Many couldn't even speak the languages of the other Earth craft involved. All was confusion, everyone shooting every which way. As we know, several, at least, of the extraterrestrials were destroyed. The rest disappeared to from whence they came, it is to be supposed, in a burst of speed beyond our own ships."

"All right," Don said, "but you don't bring into this fanciful story the fact that from time to time they come back."

"I don't believe it," Thor said.

Don was glaring at him now. "Damn it," he said, "you make less sense by the minute. They're continually being spotted. Sometimes one at a time, sometimes a small group, sometimes a larger one. What do you think our Sector Scouts are out for, fun and games, or just the ride?"

"Remember the Flying Saucers?"

"I don't know what you're talking about."

"Sometimes they called them UFOs, Unidentified Flying Objects. About the middle of the last century, a regular craze went through the United States, in particular. Hundreds and even thousands of UFOs were spotted. They were popularly assumed to be visitors from space. Some viewers went to the extreme of seeing them land and sometimes little green men, or whatever, would come out. In a few cases, crackpots would claim that they were taken aboard and flown off to Jupiter, or wherever, where, surprise, surprise, they spoke Earth languages. But to boil it down, no real proof was ever presented that these UFOs were from other worlds. They never did explain all of them, but there was never proof that they were extraterrestrial."

Don said belligerently, "Do you mean that all these patrol reports our Space Scouts send in are hysteria, or just plain lying or mistakes?"

31

"Yes, that's exactly what I'm saying."

Don said, "Sometimes our spacecraft fire on these Kradens they spot."

"Maybe they fire, and at what, I wouldn't know. But I doubt if they're firing at Kradens or any other extraterrestrials. I suspect it's largely trigger-happy space pilots, at nerve's end, or possibly touched with space cafard."

Don had another protest. "You forget that some of our ships are missing. Totally missing."

"I'm not at all surprised at accidents in space. Our ships aren't that advanced as yet. The fact that a Space Scout disappears is no proof that a Kraden destroyed it."

Don said, belligerently again, "That could happen on some occasions, but remember Vico Chu and Arch Windemere? They both reported spotting Kradens, and both reported going in to attack, and both were never seen again. We didn't even find debris from their scouts."

Thor said stubbornly, "I have a theory that they spotted each other, took each other for Kradens, panicked, both fired and destroyed each other."

"Almighty Ultimate," Don said in disgust.

Thor said, "Where in the hell do we get such names as Kradens? We've never been in any kind of contact with them whatsoever."

Don snorted. "The names just sort of materialized. Nobody seems to know who dreamed up the name Kraden for their species. But their fleet was photographed during that first action and their spaceships were different sizes, so the military gave them different names, just so they'd have some sort of label to work with."

The big man said, "At any rate, we have no particular reason to think them belligerent. For all we know, maybe they didn't want anything more than to trade."

"Trade what?" Don said in rejection. "If they can cross interstellar space, they're so far ahead of us that we couldn't have anything they want."

But the other shook his head. "Possibly they've run out of some of the more rare metals or other elements. If their civilization is far beyond our own, it's probably much older. Even in our own economy, we're running desperately short of some basic elements. For that matter, possibly they're highly cultured, and fascinated with the art and artifacts of alien cultures. Possibly they would like to pick up such little items as Leonardo da Vincis, or whatever."

"No," Don said. "It's out of the question. If there aren't any Kradens coming through any more, and they weren't even belligerent when they turned up half a century ago, it would have come out by now. A whole solar system isn't so stupid as to fight bogeymen, who don't exist, for fifty years."

The big man looked at him thoughtfully and threw his biggest bombshell. He said, "Perhaps there are elements who profit by the false alarm."

III

Don Mathers didn't leave the big man's apartment until afternoon. They'd had a huge breakfast, and by the time it was over Don had thoroughly recovered.

He asked the other guardedly about the doctor, who would provide you with a false illness that could result in your honorable discharge from the military, for free. Thor explained that he wasn't alone in opposing the all-out efforts of Earth and its solar system colonies to gird for defense against the Kradens. To him it was madness that the human race was devoting every effort to prepare for fighting an enemy that didn't exist.

"It reminds me of the race to the moon," he said in disgust.

Don said, over his coffee, "How do you mean?"

"Back in the very early days of space travel. The United States got a slow start but then dramatically announced that they were going to beat the Russians to the moon by landing there before the decade was out. Billions of dollars were spent, many of them squandered due to haste. Millions of man hours of the best scientists and technicians the country could boast were tossed into the supposed race to the moon. As a result, sure enough, they got there first and before the decade was out. The only thing was, there was no race. The Russians had made no attempt to land men on Luna. They were devoting their efforts to less frenetic experiments in establishing space platforms and sending out probes to Venus and Mars, and spending a damn sight less money and effort in doing so."

"Well," Don said, "back to this doctor."

"The doctor feels the same as I do. The whole thing's a farce. He believes that any man who devotes his career to the Space Service, or anything else connected with supposed defense, is wasting his life. And he's willing to help get anybody out who wants it. Are you interested?"

"Let me think about it," Don said evasively.

How did he know he could trust this big, seemingly generous man? He hardly knew him and the situation was a dangerous one. Theoretically, the human race was at war. Deliberate desertion could be punished with a firing squad. Suppose the doctor changed his mind, sometime in the future, and reported him. Or suppose someone else informed on the doctor and he was arrested and psyched. He'd spill everything he knew, including Thor Bjornsen's name and that of Don Mathers.

Don thanked the other again and offered to transfer some of his pseudo-dollar credits to him in payment. Thor Bjornsen laughingly refused and told him to think over the doctor's proposition. The big man was between jobs and could usually be located at the apartment. The trouble with his finding another position was that he didn't want anything even remotely connected with the war effort, and there were precious few jobs these days that weren't either directly or indirectly so connected.

Don Mathers was at loose ends. He had gone through quite a few of his pseudo-dollars the night before and so was deprived of the wherewithal to spend his three weeks leave in the manner he ordinarily would have. Besides, he was still glum about the treatment he had received from Dian Keramikou and apprehensive about the commodore and the possibility that his commander would send him to the medicos.

So he made his way to Harry's Nuevo Mexico Bar. At least he had credit there and could drink without drawing on his pseudo-dollar supply.

The bar, this early in the afternoon, was almost empty. Don spotted a fellow One Man Scout pilot on a stool and went over to join him. It was Eric Hansen, who held down a full lieutenant's rank, in spite of the fact that he was still assigned to the tiny scouts.

Don said, "Cheers, Eric. What spins?" He took the stool next to the other.

"My head," the other said gloomily. "Hi, Don. I just got in from a three week patrol and I'm hanging one on."

Harry came down and Don ordered a beer.

He said to Eric, "Didn't you spot a Kraden once?"

"Yeah. About a year ago. Big excitement. That's how I got my promotion."

"What happened?"

"Nothing happened. It was just for a couple of seconds. It looked like one of those Dorsi Class cruisers to me. Traveling like a bat out of hell. Then it disappeared."

Don glanced at him from the side of his eyes. He said, "Eric, damn it, you *sure* you saw that Kraden?"

The other was mildly indignant. "Sure I'm sure. What the hell are you talking about?"

"How long were you out when you saw it?"

"I was just about to head in. The patrol was over."

"Any space cafard at all?"

"Almighty Ultimate. Anybody's got a touch of cafard after three or four weeks in space, all alone."

Don finished his beer and made circular motions with a forefinger to request another from Harry, who came rambling down. Two strangers in civilian garb had entered and he had just waited upon them at one of the tables.

Don said to Eric, "Could it have been a hallucination?"

"What?"

"The Kraden."

Eric finished his highball with a quick gesture of the practiced drinker. He was still mildly indignant, in fact, less so than previously. He said plaintively, "Of course it could have been hallucination. I only saw it for a few seconds. Hell, in my time, I've seen elves playing around in the cockpit after a couple of weeks in deep space. So have you, no doubt."

"I usually see fairies," Don said. "Real pretty ones, with gossamer pink wings."

"You're probably a latent homosexual," Eric told him.

They sat there for a while. Eric got another drink. He said, "How long do you go on before you get the big jolt of space cafard and go completely tripe-ripe?"

"I don't know," Don said, knocking on the bar with his knuckles, though he knew damn well it wasn't wood. "What do you mean the Kraden disappeared?"

"Just that. One second it was there. Then it was gone. The only thing I can figure is that Intelligence is right. The Kradens have some way of dropping into ultra-space, or qua-space, or hyper-space, or whatever gobbledygook name you want to call it, and take off faster than light."

Don said, pulling at his drink, "Don't be drivel-happy. Nothing can go as fast as light. That's basic. You got that in training."

"I didn't say anything about traveling at the speed

of light. I said traveling faster than light. The big double domes these days are working it over. How otherwise could the Kradens come from some, uh, other star system? Hell, even the closest ones, uh, Alpha Centauri A and B are 4.3 light years from here and we haven't any reason to believe that's where they came from. The next nearest is Epsilon Eridani and that's almost eleven light years away. The Kradens *have* to have some way of traveling faster than light."

The other was getting more drenched by the minute, Don realized, but he said, impatiently, "You can't travel faster than the speed of light."

"Balls. Einstein never said so."

Don looked at him. "Where in the hell did you take your basic?"

"Einstein said you couldn't travel at the speed of light. He didn't say anything about traveling faster."

"Chum-pal, you've really got a load on. I envy you. But how could you possibly travel faster than light, without at one point traveling at the same speed as light?"

Eric said glumly, obviously tiring of the subject, "How would I know? There must be some way of dodging through the crucial point."

One of the two men who had entered and taken a table came up and said, "Are either of you gentlemen sub-lieutenant Donal Mathers?"

Don gave him the once over and said, "I am."

The newcomer was well dressed. His face was on

the pinched side and his hair was thinning, which was passingly strange since baldness had long since been cured. His lips was dark, almost bluish, and his eyes were faded and somehow evasive. He projected uncomfortableness.

The stranger said, "My name's Cockney, Frank Cockney. I wonder if I could have a few words with you, Lieutenant, over at the table." He made a gesture at the table where his companion sat.

Don instinctively didn't like him. "Why?" he said.

Cockney regarded him patiently. "You'll know that when we've had the few words, won't you? One guarantee. You won't lose any money."

"I haven't any to lose," Don said. He looked over at the table the two strangers had taken. Harry's bar didn't usually have many customers who weren't in Space Services uniform. The other sat there unperturbedly, an untouched drink before him. He was a larger man than this one, almost as large as Thor Bjornsen, but dark rather than light. His face was expressionless. For some reason, Don thought of both of them as the mobster types you saw in the old revival movie and TV shows that were all the thing these days and sent viewers into spasms of laughter.

Don said, "What the hell," and came to his feet. He went over to the table, pulled out a chair and said, "What do you want?"

The smaller of the two strangers resumed his own chair and said, "Can you prove you're sub-lieutenant Donal Mathers?" His voice was polite enough.

"Of course I can prove it. I have my Space Service I.D. and I've got my Universal Credit Card."

"May we see them, please?"

"What are you, police or something?" Don Mathers couldn't figure it out, and he didn't particularly like the looks of these two. Besides, he wanted to get back to his drink.

"No," the big one said.

Frank Cockney said, "This is Bil Golenpaul. "No, we're not police."

Don Mathers shrugged, ran a thumbnail over his mustache in irritation, but shrugged again and brought out his identification.

Cockney looked at it briefly and said, "The boss wants to see you."

Don put his papers back into his pocket and said, "Great. And who in the hell is the boss?" It came to him now that by the looks of these two, their emptiness of facial expression, they were the kind of men fated to be ordered around at the pleasure of those with wealth or brains, neither of which they had or would ever have.

"Maybe he'll tell you when he sees you," the other said, patiently and reasonably.

Don came back to his feet. He said, "Well, you can tell the boss——"

The one named Golenpaul said, "Suggest you check your pseudo-dollars credit, Lieutenant."

Don squinted at him. "Why?"

Neither of the two said anything.

In continued irritation with this whole damn thing, he brought forth his Universal Credit Card and put it in the table's slot and dialed the International Data Banks.

He said, "What is my credit standing?"

The mechanical voice answered almost immediately, "5324 pseudo-dollars and 64 cents."

Don Mathers stared at the screen. He had never had five thousand pseudo-dollars to his credit at one time in his whole life. He said finally, "When was the most recent credit deposited to my account? And how much was it?"

The screen said, "This morning. The amount was five thousand pseudo-dollars."

"Who deposited it?"

"It was transferred to your account by the Interplanetary Conglomerate."

Don Mathers had never heard of the organization. He took back his Universal Credit Card, returned it to his pocket and looked across the table at Cockney and Golenpaul. "All right," he said. "Let's go see the boss. I haven't anything else to do and his calling card intrigues me."

He waved a farewell to Eric and Harry and followed the two strangers out to the street. There was a swank helio-hover parked at the curb, to his surprise. Privately-owned vehicles weren't allowed on the surface streets of Center City.

Golenpaul sat in the pilot's place and Cockney

next to him. Don Mathers got into the back. The craft was somewhat of a sportster and had but four seats. The big man dialed their destination and the helio-hover zoomed off, immediately reaching for higher altitudes.

"So what does the boss want with me?" Don said.

Cockney said laconically, "He seldom lets us in on his business, Lieutenant."

The hi-rise Interplanetary Lines Building was evidently their destination. Don Mathers had, on occasion, been in some of the offices on the lower levels, some of the restaurants and nightspots, but they were now heading for the penthouse on the roof. They swept in to a landing on what was obviously real grass and as well-kept as a golf course.

Don began to goggle even before they emerged from the helio-hover.

It was unbelievable that they were atop a building. It had been so landscaped that it would seem to be a park. There were trees, shrubs, flowers. There was even a small stream and two Japanese bridges across it. In the center of the park, or perhaps it was better termed a wood, was a rather large Swiss-type chalet.

Cockney said, "This way."

Don followed him, still gawking at the unbelievably ostentatious surrounds.

They headed for a terrace before the chalet and as they approached Don could make out three men there, two seated in beach chairs, a portable type autobar between them. The third stood slightly back and to one side.

One of the seated men looked to be in his late middle years, the other about forty. The gentleman who was standing and looking somewhat deferential was younger, perhaps thirty-five. He was dressed in a conservative business suit, the older men were in resort wear, very informal.

Don Mathers, as he got closer, thought that he recognized the impossibly corpulent one, from a newscast, or possibly from some illustrated article. He couldn't quite place him. The fact that he was so unhealthily fat came as a surprise in this age when the medical researchers had conquered obesity. It took a fanatical gourmand not to be able to control his weight. The man looked like a latter-day Hermann Goering, his plump hands laced over his belly, his porcine eyes small in the layers of fat of his face.

The other seated one could have passed for a stereotype villain, complete to the built-in sneer. Few men, in actuality, either look like or sound like the conventionalized villain. This was an exception, Don decided. Had this one been in uniform he well could have assumed the role of a Russian general of the Second World War period. He even had a shaven head which was well tanned.

Neither of them came to their feet to greet the newcomer.

44

Don took them in carefully, before saying, "I suppose that one of you is the boss."

"That is correct," the fat one grunted. He looked at Don's two escorts and said, "Frank, you and Bil take off. Keep yourselves available, on instant call."

"Yes, Mr. Demming." Cockney all but touched his forelock. The two backed several feet before turning and heading for the helio-hover.

The younger man, still standing as though anxiously, said, "Lieutenant Mathers, this is Mr. Lawrence Demming and this is Mr. Maximilian Rostoff."

Demming was the fat one. He had been running his little eyes up and down Mathers. "Why aren't you in uniform?" he puffed.

"I'm on leave," Don told him. "What did you want to see me about?"

Demming took up a well-chilled glass that sat on a small table beside him and took a surprisingly dainty sip, considering his gross appearance.

He said, "Sit down, Lieutenant Mathers. What will you have to drink?"

Don sat and said, "Tequila."

The fat man looked at him. Maximilian Rostoff laughed contempt.

Demming said, "In my private stock, I have some genuine French cognac, if you are accustomed to spirits this time of the day."

Don said, and immediately knew he had said the wrong thing, "Real French cognac?" In all his drinking career, which had been extensive considering his age, he had tasted only the modern synthetic.

Demming said, without expression, "Yes. Laid down during the reign of Napoleon the Little."

"I'll have cognac," Don said.

The younger man, still standing, hustled forward to the autobar and dialed. He said deferentially to Demming, "The 1869, sir?"

"No," the fat man wheezed. "The 1851. The Lieutenant must get used to the better things." He smiled greasily at Don. "There are only four cases of 1851 Napoleon brandy left in existence. I have three of them."

"Thanks," Don said.

He knew who they were now, both of them. Demming was a North American, Rostoff a European by birth. Both of them were international tycoons, in fact they were interplanetary tycoons.

Neither of them seemed to be in any great hurry to get to the point. On the face of it, they were sizing him up. He hadn't the vaguest idea why.

The cognac came in a beautiful crystal snifter glass. Although he had never sampled real brandy before in his life, and certainly not in crystal, he knew the procedure from Tri-Di shows, from revived movies. He swirled the precious beverage around in the glass, cupping it so that the warmth of his hands would cause the bouquet to announce itself. He put his nose in the snifter glass and inhaled.

They were still taking him in thoughtfully.

He said, just to say something, indicating the grounds, "I'd hate to pay the rent on this place."

Demming said, offhandedly, "I own the building. I reserve the top two floors and the roof for my own establishment when I am in residence in Center City."

It had never occurred to Don Mathers that a single person would, or could, own something like the Interplanetary Lines Building. It simply hadn't occurred to him. The government, yes, perhaps even some multi-national consortium. But one man?

More and more was coming back to him about Lawrence Demming. Robber baron, he might have been branded back in the nineteenth century. Transportation and uranium baron of the solar system. Inwardly, Don Mathers snorted. Had Demming been a pig he would have been butchered long since.

Rostoff said, "You have identification?"

Once again Don Mathers fumbled through his pockets and came up with his Universal Credit Card and his military I.D. Both of them examined the papers with care, front and back.

Demming huffed and said, "Your papers indicate that you pilot a One Man Scout. What sector do you patrol, Lieutenant?"

Don took a sip of his superlative brandy and looked at the corpulent man over his glass. "That's military information, Mr. Demming."

Demming made a moue with his plump lips. "Did Frank Cockney reveal to you the five thousand pseudo-dollars that have been deposited to your account?" He didn't wait for an answer but added, "You took it. Either return it, or tell me what sector you patrol, Lieutenant."

Don Mathers was well aware of the fact that a man of Demming's position wouldn't have to go to over much effort to acquire such information, anyway. It wasn't of particular importance and, of course, the magnate had strings going into the very highest echelons of the Octagon.

He shrugged and said, "A22-K223. I fly the V-102."

Maximilian Rostoff handed back the identification papers to Don and said to his colleague, after checking a solar system sector chart, "You were right, Demming. He's the man."

Demming shifted his great bulk and his beach chair and took up his cordial glass again. He sipped it daintily and said, "Very well. How would you like to hold the Galactic Medal of Honor, Lieutenant Mathers?"

IV

Don Mathers laughed sarcastically. "How would you?" he said.

The fat tycoon scowled. "I am not jesting, Lieutenant Mathers. I never jest. I considered it, but for various reasons I do not believe it practical. Obviously, I am not of the military. It would be quite unusual if not impossible for me to gain such an award. But you are the pilot of a One Man Scout. I also lack the charisma. You are young, moderately handsome and have a certain air of dash about you. You would make a very popular holder of the Galactic Medal of Honor."

Don said, disgust in his voice, "I've got just about as much chance of winning the Galactic Medal of Honor as I have of giving birth to triplets."

The transportation and uranium magnate wiggled a disgustingly fat finger at him and said, "I'll arrange for it, in collaboration with my colleague, here, Mr. Rostoff."

Don Mathers gawked at him. He blurted finally,

"Like hell you will. There's not enough money in the solar system to fiddle with the awarding of the Galactic Medal of Honor. There comes a point, Demming, where even your kind of bread can't carry the load. Corruption we might have, on all levels of government, but it doesn't touch the Galactic Medal of Honor. And it never will. The people wouldn't stand for it."

Demming settled back in his chair again, laced his fat hands over his belly, closed his eyes and said, "Dirck, brief us on the space defenses of the solar system."

The neat, quiet young man who had been hovering in the background, stepped forward. He was a bland-faced type with secretary written all over him. Although seemingly alert and ever ready to obey, his eyes had a disconcerting empty quality. And his mouth was not the type to indulge in smiling.

He said, in a brisk voice, "Yes, sir. The patroling spacecraft have major bases on Earth, Luna and Mars. There are smaller bases on the Jupiter satellites, Io, Europa, Ganymede and Callisto. There is another base on the Saturn satellite Titan. When the planetary engineering problems have been worked out, there are plans to establish another base on the Neptune satellite Triton. The One and Two Men Scouts patrol nearest to their home bases, and for the shortest periods. They are the last line of warning, in case a Kraden sneaks through. Beyond them, in scantier numbers, are Destroyers holding four men. The Destroyers stay out for as long as two months at a time. Beyond them, are eight to ten men Light Cruisers, which stay out for as much as three months at a time. They are the first warning and are expected to stand and fight in case Kradens appear. These are all warning craft. Nearer in, closer to Earth and the other bases, are the Monitors. They are continually in orbit, having been built in space and quite impossible to land due to their size. They have a crew of approximately thirty. Fresh crews are sent up to them every six months to relieve them. They are the heavies, ready to zero-in on the enemy when and if the Kradens get through the initial defense. Also in the defense screen are the Space Platforms, the permanent artificial satellites which are hardly maneuverable at all but carry the heaviest of our defenses, short of those based on Earth itself. In all, the Solar System defenses include at least twenty thousand spacecraft, not to mention the permanent installations on Earth, Luna, Mars and the Jupiter and Saturn satellites. More than a billion men and women are in the armed forces."

The secretary came to an end.

Don said, "Is any of that supposed to be news to me?"

Demming ignored that and muttered, his eyes still closed, "Thank you, Dirck. Max?"

The other magnate took over after taking a swallow from the glass of sparkling wine before him. He

51

looked at Don calculatingly and said, "A few days ago, Mr. Demming and I flew in from Io in his private space yacht, accompanied only by his secretary here, Dirck Bosch. The yacht is completely automated, without crew. As a matter of fact, I am sorry Mr. Demming was along, and he is sorry I was along. It required that we become partners when we made our discovery."

Don said, "Look, could I have another cognac?" A feeling of excitement was growing within him and the drinks he'd had earlier had worn away. Something very big, very, very big, was developing. He hadn't the vaguest idea what it might be.

The secretary stepped forward and dialed the fresh drink.

Maximilian Rostoff ran a hand back over his bald pate and went on, saying, "Lieutenant, how would you like to capture a Kraden cruiser? If I am not incorrect, the Space Service calls them Miro Class."

Don laughed nervously, not getting it, not knowing where the other was at but still feeling the growing excitement. He said, "In the whole history of the war between our races, we've never captured a Kraden ship intact, or even remotely so. It would help a lot if we could. Our engineers would like to get their hands on one."

Rostoff said, "This one isn't exactly intact, but it's nearly so."

Don looked from Rostoff to Demming and then

back again. He said, "What in the hell are you talk-ing about?"

Rostoff nodded, as though that was a reasonable question. "In your sector," he said, "we ran into a derelict Miro Class Kraden cruiser. The crew—re-pulsive-looking creatures—were all dead, some forty of them in all. Mr. Demming and I assumed that the spacecraft had been hit during one of the actions be-tween our ships and theirs and that somehow both sides had failed to recover the wreckage. At any rate, today it is floating, abandoned of all life, in your sector. The Almighty Ultimate only knows why it hasn't been detected by radar, or whatever, long before this." He added softly, "One has to approach quite close, except from the angle we first saw it from, before any signs of battle are evident. The spaceship looks intact."

Lawrence Demming opened his porker eyes again, smiled flatly and said, "And that is the cruiser you are going to capture, Lieutenant."

Don Mathers bolted his new brandy and licked a final drop from the edge of his lip. He said. "And why should that rate the most difficult decoration that we've ever instituted?"

"Don't be dense," Rostoff told him, his tone grat-ing mockery. "Capture isn't actually the term. You're going to radio in, reporting a Miro Class Kraden cruiser. We assume that your superiors will order you to stand off, that help is coming, that your tiny

One Man Scout isn't large enough to do anything more than to keep the enemy under observation until a squadron arrives. But you will radio back that they are escaping and that you plan to attack. When your reinforcements arrive, Lieutenant, you will have conquered the Kraden, single-handed, against odds of—what would you say—fifty to one?"

Don Mathers' mouth was dry, his palms moist. He said, "A One Man Scout against a Miro Class cruiser? At least five hundred to one, Mr. Rostoff. At least."

Demming grunted. "There would be little doubt of your being awarded the Galactic Medal of Honor, Lieutenant, especially in view of the fact that Colin Casey is dead and there isn't a living bearer of the award. The powers that be in Space Command like to have a bearer of the Galactic Medal of Honor around—it's good for solar system morale. Dirck, another drink for the Lieutenant."

Don said, "Look. Why? I think you might be right about getting the decoration. But why, and why me, and what's your percentage?"

Demming muttered heavily, "You are a perceptive young man, Lieutenant Mathers. Obviously, Mr. Rostoff and I have an iron or two in the fire. We now get to the point." He settled back in his chair again, closed his eyes again, obviously waiting for his partner to take back over.

Maximilian Rostoff leaned forward, his lupine face very serious. He said, "Lieutenant, the exploitation of the Jupiter satellites, in particular, is in the very earliest stages. There is every reason to believe that the new sources of radioactives on Callisto alone may mean the needed power edge that might give us victory over the Kradens when they appear again. Whether or not that is so, someone is going to make literally billions out of this new frontier. Possibly as much as a trillion."

"I still don't see——"

"Lieutenant Mathers," Rostoff interrupted patiently, "the bearer of the Galactic Medal of Honor is above law. He carries with him an inalienable prestige of such magnitude that . . . well, let me use an example. Suppose a bearer of the Galactic Medal of Honor formed a stock corporation to exploit the pitchblende of Callisto. How difficult would it be for him to dispose of the stock? How difficult for him to get concessions from the government?"

Demming grunted and without bothering to open his eyes said, "And suppose that there were a few, ah, crossed wires in the manipulation of the corporations's business?" He sighed deeply. "Believe me, Lieutenant Mathers, there are an incredible number of laws which have accumulated down through the centuries to hamper the businessman. It is a continual fight to be able to carry on at all. The ability to do no legal wrong would be priceless in the development of the new frontier." He sighed again, so deeply as to make his bulk quiver. "Priceless."

Rostoff laid it on the line. "We are offering you a partnership, Mathers. You, with your Galactic Medal of Honor, will be our front man. Mr. Demming and I will supply the initial capital to get underway, the organization and the know-how, the brains. We'll take Callisto and the other satellite colonies the way Grant took Richmond, to use the old Americanism."

Don said slowly, looking down at the empty glass he was twirling in his fingers, "Look, we're in a war to the death with the Kradens. In the long run it's either us or them. At a time like this you're suggesting that we fake an action that will eventually enable us to milk the new satellites to the tune of billions."

Demming grunted meaninglessly.

Don said, "The theory is that all men, all of us, ought to have our shoulders to the wheel. This project sounds to me as though we'd be throwing rocks under it."

Demming closed his eyes, still again.

Rostoff took up the bottle of sparkling wine from the ice bucket next to him and poured the drink into his champagne glass. He said to Don Mathers, "Lieutenant, it's a dog-eat-dog socioeconomic system we live under. If we eventually defeat the Kradens, one of the very reasons will be because we are a dog-eat-dog society. Every man for himself and the devil take the hindmost. Our apologists dream up some beautiful gobbledygook phrases for it, such as free enterprise, but actually it's dog-eat-dog. Surprisingly enough, the system works, or at least it has so far. It leads to progress, the inept fall out of the game. Right now, the human race needs the radioactives of the Jupiter satellites. In acquiring them, somebody is going to make a tremendous amount of money. Why shouldn't it be us?"

Don said, a dogged quality in his voice, "Why not, if you—or we—can do it honestly?"

Demming's grunt was nearer to a snort this time.

Rostoff said sourly, "Don't be naive, Lieutenant. Whoever does it, is going to need little integrity. You don't win in a sharper's card game by playing your cards honestly. The biggest sharper wins. We've just found a joker somebody dropped on the floor. If we don't use it, we're suckers."

Demming opened his pig eyes and said, "All this is on the academic side. We checked your background thoroughly before approaching you, Mathers. We know your record, even before you entered the Space Service, your, ah, minor peccadilloes. Just between the three of us, wouldn't you like out of your commission? There are a full billion men and women in our armed forces—you can be spared. Let us say that you've already done your share. Can't you see the potentialities in spending the rest of your life with the Galactic Medal of Honor in your pocket?"

Don said, breathing a little harder, "If it came out, it would mean the firing squad for all of us."

The fat man was reasonable. "How could it come out? Only we three would be in on it, and it is certainly not to the interest of any of us to reveal anything."

Don looked at the secretary. "How about him? You're not even cutting him in, and he knows the whole thing."

Demming shook his head. "Dirck is completely faithful to me. He's my man."

Don said, "I'll have to think about it."

Maximilian Rostoff said, "Don't take too long about thinking. Every day that goes by runs the risk that someone else might also spot the derelict." He looked at his wrist chronometer and stood. "I've got a corporation board meeting," he said. "Demming, I'll leave it to you to give the Lieutenant any details—how to get in touch with us, the exact location of the Kraden spaceship, and so forth."

He brought his transceiver from a jacket pocket, opened it, activated it and spoke a few words. Within a minute, a luxurious helio-hover had swooped in and a uniformed chauffeur had popped out to open the door.

Rostoff repeated, "Don't take too long about it, Lieutenant." He turned and headed for his craft.

Demming said, "What time is it, Dirck?"

The secretary said promptly, seemingly without having to check, "Ten minutes until two, sir."

The fat man lurched to his feet. He wheezed to Don Mathers, "Why not stay for dinner? Perhaps it would be interesting for you to experience the way of life you could become used to if you bore the Galactic Medal of Honor."

"Why . . . thank you," Don said, standing too.

Lawrence Demming waddled, rather than walked, toward the chalet, Don Mathers following. As soon as they left the area where they had been drinking and talking, two liveried servants materialized and began policing it up. Dirck Bosch, the secretary headed in a different direction toward the chalet. As hired help, he seemingly did not eat with the boss.

Don said to his host, "I still don't like the idea of his being in on the whole story. Just one slip and we'd be sunk—if I come in with you."

Demming grunted. "I have Dirck under my thumb. I know where the body is buried, as the saying goes. I own him, body and soul."

"Sometimes a worm turns under too much pressure," Don said, still unhappy.

"Not this worm," the fat man said, leading the way into the chalet proper.

It was a new experience for Don Mathers. Like everyone else, he had been surfeited all his life with the luxurious sets of films, TV and now Tri-Di. Nine shows out of ten were devoted to characters who lived on a scale of luxury unknown to ninety-nine percent of the population. Evidently, that was what the viewers wanted, a dream world, a fairyland world.

But Don Mathers had never seen anything like
this, even on Tri-Di. This was a museum. Obviously,
the uncouth Lawrence Demming had had little to
say about its decor. Undoubtedly, the interior decorator had been the best available; undoubtedly, the
budget for art had been absolutely unlimited. Don
Mathers was no great connoisseur of art but he recognized paintings that he vaguely thought were in
various of the world's museums. How had the interplanetary magnate ever acquired them?

Possibly, Don decided sourly, by buying the museum.

He had expected to be conducted to the dining
room, but instead was taken to an elevator.

Demming said heavily, "We rough it up here for
the sun, fresh air and so forth, but actually we usually live below."

If this was roughing it, in Don Mathers' considered opinion, then by the same standards you could
have consigned Nefertiti, Cleopatra and Madame Du
Barry to the rank of two-dollar whores. The rugs
they had waded through must be Persian, and antiques, he realized, though he knew nothing of rugs.
He knew nothing of furniture, either, but surely this
was all of museum quality, and, he supposed, at
least several centuries old. For Don Mathers'
money it didn't look particularly comfortable.

They entered the spacious elevator, Demming
muttering something about being hungry. The mag-

nate spoke into the elevator screen and they descended sedately. Then the elevator stopped and then shunted sideward for a distance Mathers couldn't calculate. It stopped again and then started off in another direction; forty-five degrees, he estimated, in the alteration of course. What in the hell kind of an elevator was this? It stopped again, momentarily, and then began to descend once more. Finally it came to a complete halt and the door slid open.

They emerged into a dining room.

At first, Don was mildly surprised at its size. He had expected, from what he had seen thus far, some absolutely baronial room. This was large but not as much so as all that. The table was set for four, and possibly could have accommodated eight, but no more in comfort.

Demming mumbled, "Family dining room. Cozy, eh?"

Cozy wasn't quite the word. Still again, though no connoisseur of art, Don Mathers recognized that the room was done in Picasso, the twentieth century master.

Demming saw the direction of his eyes and said, "My daughter's a collector. Can't stand the man myself. Lot of curd. Could do better myself, Pay off the national debt of France, at the time he lived, for what they cost."

There were two women at the far side of the room

61

and the interplanetary magnate led Don over to them. They were in semi-formal afternoon dress and both had small sherry glasses in hand.

Demming said, "My dear, may I present sub-lieutenant Donal Mathers? My wife, Martha, Lieutenant."

Don Mathers had taken the usual course in etiquette at the Space Forces Academy, which supposedly turned out gentlemen as well as fighting pilots. He bent over Mrs. Demming's hand.

She was completely unattractive, colorless and bland of expression. She even had slightly buck teeth and Don could only wonder why she hadn't had them straightened as a child; dental science had advanced as much as any other field of medicine and a mouth full of perfect teeth was assumed in everyone. He vaguely remembered reading something about her once. The Demming fortune went back several generations and the tycoon had inherited wealth beyond the dreams of most men, but when he had married the heiress Martha Wentworth his fortune had doubled. Looking at her, Don wondered inwardly if it had been worth it.

Demming said, "And this is my daughter Alicia, Lieutenant."

Now Alicia was another thing and Don wondered how such a woman as Martha Demming could ever have produced her. Her eyes were a startling green and her skin was flawlessly tanned an even gold that looked theatrical and almost implausible. Her hair was long, down to her shoulders, blond, rich and pale. Her figure, too, was rich, though possibly just a shade underweight.

She didn't offer to shake hands. She said, "A sub-lieutenant? What in the world do you do, Lieutenant?"

Don said, "I pilot a One Man Scout."

"Good heavens," she said, her nose slightly high, as though there was an odor about. "Father does bring home the strangest people."

"That will be all, Alicia," Demming sighed. "The lieutenant is a most perceptive young man." And to Don. "Would you like an Amontillado before we eat?"

"Amontillado?"

"The driest of the Spanish sherries. I put down quite a few pipes before they discontinued the wineries."

"Oh. Well, no thanks. I suppose I got a sufficient edge on from the cognac."

The fat man looked at the women and gestured to the table. "Then, my dears. . . ."

Don was seated across from Alicia. She was so startlingly attractive that it was difficult to keep his eyes off her. She, however, seemed completely oblivious to his masculine charm. Alicia obviously did not mingle with ranks as low as sub-lieutenant.

Miraculously, liveried servants materialized. Two stood behind each chair. Two silver ice buckets were brought and placed immediately to the side of Demming. A long green bottle was brought forth, deftly wrapped in a napkin, deftly opened. The servant had a gold key suspended about his neck. He poured half a glass of wine into a crystal goblet before Demming and took a step backward respectfully.

The fat tycoon swirled the wine a bit to bring up the bouquet, then sipped. He pursed his plump lips thoughtfully.

The *sommelier* said, anxiety in his voice, "Perhaps the Gewurztraminer instead? It has come of age and should be supreme, sir."

Demming shook his head and said, "No, no, Alfredo. The Riesling is still excellent, though in another six months or so we may have another story."

The servant served the two ladies, then Don, and returned to fill his master's glass, then put the bottle back into the ice bucket. There were two other similar bottles.

Meanwhile, another lackey had pushed an hors d'oeuvre cart up beside Martha Demming. On it was a variety sufficient to feed a hungry squad of infantrymen. She selected exactly one canape and the cart moved on to Alicia.

Demming indicated the wine to Don. "Edelbeerensauslese Riesling," he said.

Don tasted and blinked. He said, "But, it's real wine."

"Yes, of course," the other said in fat satisfaction, and taking another sizable swig. The wine waiter was there immediately to refill the glass to the two thirds level.

Don said, in puzzlement, "But I thought that the government had terminated wine grapes so that the acreage could be devoted· to more necessary produce."

Demming leered smugly. "I prevailed upon the authorities to allow me to continue production on small, but the very best, vineyards in France, Germany, Italy and Hungary, in the name of retaining an art that has come down through the centuries. My vineyards, then, are in the way of being museums. A manner of maintaining a tradition." He winked one of his pig eyes. "Even the President often dines with me and appreciates my vintages." He chuckled heavily. "He wouldn't dare serve wine in his own palace. The outcry in such areas as what we once called France, would reach the skies, if they knew his privilege."

The hors d'oeuvre cart had reached Don Mathers.

Demming pointed out several, judiciously. "I can recommend Choux au Caviar Mimosa."

One of the waiters behind Don's chair immediately served the guest two puffs overflowing with gray-black fish eggs.

Don looked blank. "Caviar?" he said. "I've read about it but I didn't know it was still being produced."

Demming said, "I have my own artificial lake in the Caspian Mountains. It's stocked with sturgeons and produces sufficient roe to provide me and some of my closest associates. And you must try some of this Anchovy Garlic Canape and a bit of this Pistachio Cheese Roll."

Don's plate was soon overflowing. He couldn't have eaten this much food even if nothing else was to come. He looked from the side of his eyes at Alicia's plate. She had selected three small tasties.

When the cart got to Demming it was another thing. He not only selected more than he had recommended to Don, but half again as much.

Course followed course, each with a different wine. Soup, shellfish, poultry—in this case, wild duck. Where in the hell did you get wild duck these days? Don thought. All came with various vegetable dishes, done up in such a way that sometimes Don couldn't recognize the vegetables. He was surfeited before he had finished the sauteed soft-shell crabs.

The women ate moderately, especially Alicia, who also no more than sipped at the continuing selection of wines. Don sipped too. He had done his share of sampling the Riesling and the rosé that went with the shellfish but gave up when it came to the heavier and heavier reds. He felt he was rapidly becoming drenched. Now he realized that he never should have taken those three cognacs earlier.

The climax came when one of the servants brought in an enormous platter of meat and placed it before the billionaire interplanetary tycoon, whose eyes lit up.

"Ah," he said, all but drooling. "Carré d'Agneau à la Boulangère." He looked at Don. "Do you like broiled rack of lamb?"

"Not today," Don said definitely.

The women also refused.

There must have been six to eight pounds of the rack of lamb. As Don sat there, staring in fascination, the glutton ate all of it save scraps.

As he messily tore the meat apart and gorged himself with it, he made conversation with Don Mathers.

"When are you due for your next patrol?"

"In three weeks."

The pig eyes narrowed. "Couldn't you, ah, volunteer to go out sooner?"

"They'd consider it strange," Don said.

The other swigged down heavy Burgundy before returning to the lamb.

"Why?"

"I doubt if in the history of One Man Scouts any pilot has volunteered to go out before ordered. It's not so bad, possibly, in the bigger spacecraft but the One Man Scouts are breeding grounds for space cafard."

"So," Demming said, around a bone which he had

in his fat hands and was greasing his mouth with, "it'll be three weeks before you head out?"

"Yes," Don said.

"Head out where?" Alicia said, disinterestedly.

"Into deep space," Don said, viewing Lawrence Demming. "Looking for Kradens."

V

When Don Mathers reported for duty following his standard three weeks leave of absence, it was to find a message to report to Commodore Walt Bernklau.

It hadn't been the easiest three weeks he had ever spent. His mind had been in a state of agitation. As a matter of fact, he had never actually given Demming and Rostoff a definite answer. Had there been any way of substituting someone else to "discover" and "destroy" the Kraden cruiser without doubt they would have done it, and had Don Mathers eliminated so that he couldn't expose the scheme. Don had no doubt that both of them had men on their payrolls who would do anything, literally, up to and including murder. But the thing was, nobody but Don Mathers would do. The derelict Kraden spaceship was drifting in his sector. Only he would normally discover it. It had been a far-out fluke that the two interplanetary magnates and Deming's secretary had come across the cruiser on their way between Io and Earth. No, it was either Don Mathers or nobody.

But he burned hot and cold. The stakes were so damnably high, but the risks went with them. There wasn't the chance of an icicle on Mercury but that he would be shot if the scheme was revealed. Demming and Rostoff possibly might buy their way out; without doubt they had a number of politicians on their payrolls. But not a sub-lieutenant in the Space Service. They'd court-martial and shoot him before the week was out.

He dismissed the automated hovercab which had brought him out to the base, summoned one of the hovercarts and dialed the Space Command Headquarters of the Third Division.

He duplicated the route he had taken the last time he had reported to the commodore, duplicated the snappy salute to his commanding officer when he was finally before him.

The commodore, wearing his usual weary air, looked down into his desk screen. He said, "Sub-lieutenant Donald Mathers' material, please."

He scrutinized the screen for a time before looking up to say, "Since your report on your last aborted patrol, Lieutenant, I've had some second thoughts."

"Yes, sir."

"It occurs to me that you're rather badly in need of a psych. I've gone over your record in some detail."

Don said, trying to hide the desperation in his voice, "Sir, I'd like to avoid that, if I can."

The other was impatient. He shifted his small body in his swivel chair and said, "Lieutenant, there is a good deal of superstitious nonsense about the effects of being psyched. Ninety-five percent of those who are thus treated have no negative results. Even those who react adversely usually recover eventually."

Like hell they did, Don Mathers told himself. He had seen some of the walking zombies. Even those who supposedly successfully took the treatment were never again quite the same. Something was gone out of them. Oh, sure, they became dependable pilots again. If anything, more dependable, more efficient than those who had never been psyched. But something was gone out of them. He knew that elements in the upper echelons of the Space Service were advocating that every pilot in the fleet be given the treatment for the sake of added efficiency. But thus far the action hadn't been taken. It was well known that the top brass, perfectly willing to psych lowly pilots, were not volunteering to go through the process themselves.

He said stiffly, "Sir, I would like the opportunity to prove that I don't need a psych."

The commodore was irritated. "Very well, Lieutenant. It is seldom ordered, though there are exceptions. Ordinarily, it is more or less of a voluntary thing taken on when a pilot realizes he has irrevocably shot his efficiency and patriotically wishes to return to top form."

"Yes, sir."

"Very well, Lieutenant Mathers. Carry on." The commodore twisted his mouth in a grim smile. "From this patrol I do not expect you to return before your full three weeks, Mathers. Dismissed."

"Yes, sir."

With a sinking relief in his stomach, Don turned and marched from the office. Out in the corridors, he let air from his lungs. That had been a close one.

He took his hovercart over to the officers' quarters and changed into the coveralls which were universally worn in space. He left his papers and wrist chronometer in the locker. He went on back to the hovercart and took it out to the hangers to find that his V-102, his One Man Scout, had already been wheeled out. Several of the mechanics of his crew were giving it a last minute inspection.

He came up to the sergeant who was head of the crew and said, "How does she look, Wilkins?"

Sergeant Jerry Wilkins was an old hand. Theoretically, he could have retired but he was wedded to the job and as good a mechanic as any on the base. Wilkins could have taken apart and reassembled a One Man Scout in the dark.

Don was aware of the fact that the mechanic knew that nothing had been wrong with the V-102 on the last patrol and probably nothing on the preceding three aborted patrols. But the sergeant must have had a certain tolerance. He was too long in the Space Service not to be aware of the reality of space cafard and the fact that at one time or another there wasn't a pilot who hadn't been hit by it.

Wilkins was rubbing grease from his hands with a piece of waste. He said, with satisfaction, "Lieutenant, you won't have no trouble with her this patrol. We been working her over for the last three weeks. We've got her tuned like a chronometer."

"Good," Don said. "I've been beginning to think I was hexed." He knew that the other knew he was lying, but you had to make the effort.

He was a bit behind time, due to his interview with the commodore but Don didn't allow that to hurry him. He circled the V-102, the sergeant walking behind. Care was the essence, making the difference between getting back to where he started or blowing the ultra-hot little One Man Scout. He checked, checked, checked. Then he got in and settled down into the pilot seat. Once you were space borne in a One Man Scout there was no way of getting out until you returned to base. The larger craft, yes, the Monitors and even the smaller cruisers had lifeboats, but not a One Man Scout. If something happened to you in deep space, you were dead, period.

Now, automatically, he went over the procedure that was second nature to him. He began checking in one corner of the cockpit and went around it, missing nothing. Every switch, every meter, every screen, the cooling rheostats and the cabin pressurization, every gauge.

He said finally to Wilkins, through the hatch, "All right, Sergeant, let's get this beetle into space." He closed the hatch, dogged it down, knowing the sergeant was doing the same outside.

He could envision the ground crew driving up the lift and shortly the V-102 was being hoisted up onto it. He could feel the slow-moving vehicle trudging him over to the shuttlecraft and then the V-102 being lifted up into the cradle.

He switched on his communication screen. Lieutenant Risseeuw was piloting the shuttle. "Cheers, Jan," Don said, "what spins?"

Jan Risseeuw said, "Hi, Don. Heard you've had trouble the last few patrols."

"Yeah," Don said, keeping his voice glum. "A regular jinx. If I don't snap out of this, they'll fire me and I'll have to take a job being a Tri-Di star, or something."

"Ha," the other said. "All set down there?"

"Take her away," Don said.

He knew damn good and well that Jan, as much so as his sergeant mechanic, knew—as did every pilot on the base—that Don Mathers was running scared, aborting patrol after patrol. And nobody could possibly like it. Fellow pilots tried to take care of their own, but the Space Service just wasn't large enough to run sufficient patrols. More spacecraft were being poured into the skies, but there still weren't enough. When Don Mathers was taking his three weeks leave of absence, after each patrol, his sector was empty. Command tried to cover by having his adjoining sectors manned during that period, in the same way as when he was on patrol while the adjoining pilots were on leave; but it still left a hole. And particularly did it leave a hole when a One Man Scout returned from a supposed three week patrol in just several days.

But that wasn't his worry now.

Jan lifted and Don Mathers sunk back into his acceleration chair. This was the part he, and every other pilot, particularly hated—the initial lift into space. Among other things, this was where most of the danger was. If you were going to blow, four times out of five it was when you were lifting off, getting into initial orbit.

As always, they went up fast, out into the zone where it was safe for him to activate his nuclear engines. Out where Earth was no longer in danger, even if he blew.

Don said into the screen, "How's Grete?"

"She's all right," Jan told him. "Going to drop her kid in about two weeks."

"How many does that make?"

"Four."

"Fifty years ago they could have jailed you."

"That was before the Kradens. Now we need every human being we can get. When this planetary

75

engineering really gets under way, we can populate Luna, Mars, the Jupiter satellites, maybe even some of the others."

"That's the dream," Don said. "Read the other day that they've located several asteroids that are solid ice. What they want to do is chivy them over and drop them onto Mars to melt."

"Sounds pretty far out. I'd hate to be under it when one of them dropped. But if they could swing it, it'd be something. I suppose you'd have as much water as a good-sized lake."

Don said, "I was pretty well holed up this last three weeks. Anything new happened during that time?"

"Not much. Marty Cantine reported he saw a Kraden over in his sector. Just a quick spotting and then it was gone."

"Did he?"

Don could hear the other's yawn. "Naw. When he got in, he was shaking with cafard. That boy ought to take the psych treatment."

Don said carefully, "I ran into a guy the other day, a technician on the Luna radio telescopes, who claims there aren't any Kradens. His theory is that they came that one time, half a century ago, found we were hostile, and took off and haven't returned."

Jan grunted. "He might be right. *I've* never spotted one of the bastards."

"How could you, in a shuttle?"

Jan said, "I was in the Two Man Scouts for a

couple of years. They pulled me out. Too suscepti-
ble to space cafard. They decided that not even a
psych job would help for any length of time. Well,
here we are, Don. Ready for the drop?"

"All set. See you, Jan. Give my regards to Grete."

"Luck," the shuttle pilot said.

Don could feel his craft falling away. For the moment, he was in free fall. His practiced hands
darted about the cockpit, firing up his nuclear engines.

Under way, he turned to his navigation, flicking
this, touching that, checking dials and gauges, getting the coordinates of his sector A22-K223 into the
computer. He flicked his acceleration over to 2 Gs
and felt himself pressed back into the acceleration
chair.

Don Mathers was an old hand. He reached into
his kit and brought forth a vacuum bottle. It supposedly contained fruit juice, and didn't. He took a
deep swig from it and then turned to his mini-tapes
and selected one, a revival of an old-old two dimen-
sional movie, *Gone With the Wind* and relaxed. He
enjoyed the old films, totally unbelievable though
they were.

It was a far cry from the early days of the space
age when with rocket engines you lifted off from
Earth and headed for, say, Luna. You reached your
escape velocity and from then on, until it was time
to start braking, you coasted. No more, with the
coming of nuclear powered engines. Now you could

continue to accelerate until you reached almost to your destination. Aside from the speed, you also avoided the misery of free fall. Once arrived in his sector, he'd drop it down to one G. It was a bit on the complicated side, but the double domes had worked it out over the years.

Maximilian Rostoff had evidently been a space pilot in his youth. When he and Demming had spotted the drifting Kraden derelict he had not only gotten a fix on it but had determined its course and speed and now Don had little difficulty in locating the Miro Class cruiser.

And there it was all right, drifting comparatively slowly, inertia maintaining the speed that it must have been under when it was hit and the crew killed.

He had never seen a Kraden spaceship before, though, like every other cadet, when he was at the Space Academy he had pored over the photographs and video-tapes taken during the initial battle between the Kradens and Earthmen. There could be no doubt of its extraterrestrial origin. Earth spaceships, even the Monitors which were assembled in space, were still built, for unknown reasons so far as he was concerned, to resemble overgrown torpedoes. The Kradens were built every which way and sometimes basically resembled a box.

The Miro Class cruisers looked more or less like a rectangular box. The only manner in which you could tell if they were coming or going was that there was a control area in the prow, a blister. Or, at least, that's what the Earthling technicians had decided it was, and were probably wrong, Don thought.

He braked to the speed of the other ship and then used his directional jets to circle it. It was even larger than an Earth Monitor and must have been one hell of a fighting machine in its day. If it *had* been a warcraft. According to Thor Bjornsen, it might have been a colonizing ship, or a merchantman.

Had he done a more thorough job of his patrol, the last time—hell, for the last half dozen times—he should have stumbled upon it himself. In actuality, largely he had kept himself doped up on soma during those few days he had remained in space, keeping himself only alert enough to be able to make his routine reports. Anything to fight off the space cafard.

He circled it again. If he had spotted it on his last patrol there was no doubt that he would have at first reported it as an active enemy cruiser. Demming and Rostoff had been right. The Kraden ship looked untouched by battle.

That is, if you approached it from starboard and slightly abaft the beam. From that angle, in particular, it looked untouched.

Demming and Rostoff had mentioned going inside and finding repulsive looking alien corpses. On the face of it, it had probably been Rostoff alone who made the spacewalk between the automated space yacht they were in and the extraterrestrial ship. Demming couldn't have gotten into a spacesuit, even had he wanted to. And even though he'd had constructed a special one to fit his bulk, Don doubted that the fat slob would have exerted himself to that point—no matter what the potential profitable possibilities.

He imagined that Maximilian Rostoff had warped the space yacht up against the alien craft and had then donned a spacesuit and crossed over to explore it. Don wasn't going to be able to do the equivalent. His One Man Scout boasted no spacesuit nor was there any manner of exit and entry, once in space. He would have liked to explore the interior, as Rostoff had done, but there was simply no way.

In actuality, until this point he had made no decisions. He was still in a position to report in to the base, to reveal that he had located a derelict Kraden cruiser. Undoubtedly, it would do him a lot of good. The engineers would fall all over themselves. It might even win him a promotion. Eric Hansen had been bounced up to full lieutenant just on the strength of having *seen* a Kraden—and he wasn't even positive of that.

Surely, this discovery would take the commodore off his neck, at least for the time. It would also mean that as soon as he had made the report he would be ordered to return to base. They'd want to question him in detail. He wouldn't have to stay out the full three weeks, which he dreaded.

But that wasn't all of it. Once the initial excitement was over, and he had been a several week news item, he'd be back in the same spot as before. He'd be sent out again, and when he panicked, under cafard, sooner or later the commodore would lower the boom on him. Psych.

That's what decided him. If he was psyched, it would come out that it hadn't really been him who had discovered the Kraden but Demming and Rostoff. *If* he lived to be psyched. He had no doubts at all but that the two interplanetary tycoons would put musclemen after him the moment he revealed the Miro Class cruiser to Space Command as a drifting derelict. They'd have to take steps to eliminate him, or they'd be in the soup when their scheme came out.

He dropped back into the exact position he had decided upon, took another long swig out of his vacuum bottle, then flicked the switch on his screen.

A base lieutenant's face illuminated it. He yawned and looked questioningly at Don Mathers. He said, "Mathers, your routine report isn't due for another six hours. Don't tell me you're having engine trouble again. The commodore told me——"

Don said, allowing a touch of excitement in his voice, "Mathers, Scout V-102, Sector A22-K223——"

"Yeah, yeah," the other said, still yawning. "I

know who the hell you are and where you are."

Don said excitedly, "I've spotted a Kraden cruiser! Miro Class, I think."

The lieutenant flashed into movement. He slapped a button before him. The screen in Don's One Man Scout blinked a moment and then Commodore Walt Bernklau was there.

He snapped, "Mathers, you aren't in space cafard, are you?"

"No, sir! It's a Kraden all right!"

The screen flickered again. Then it was halved. Besides the commodore, a gray haired fleet admiral looked up from the papers on his desk.

"Yes?" he said impatiently.

Don Mathers rapped, "Miro Class Kraden in section A22-K223, sir. I'm lying about two hundred kilometers off. Undetected thus far—I think. Otherwise he would have blasted me out of space. He hasn't fired on me . . . yet, at least."

The admiral was already doing things with his hands. Two subalterns came within range of his screen, took orders, dashed off. The admiral was rapidly firing commands into two other screens. After a moment, he looked up at Don Mathers again.

"Hang on, Lieutenant. Keep him under observation as long as you can. Don't get any closer. We don't want him to spot you. What are your exact coordinates?"

Don gave them to him and waited.

The commodore, still on his half of the screen,

said, suspiciously, "You're sure about this, Mathers?"

"Yes, sir!"

Within a minute, the Admiral returned to him. "Let's take a look at it, Lieutenant."

Don Mathers adjusted the screen to relay the Kraden cruiser. His palms were moist now, but everything was going to plan. He wished the hell he could have another drink.

The admiral said in excitement, "Miro Class, all right. Don't get too close, Lieutenant. You're well within range. They'll blast you to hell and gone. We're sending up three full squadrons of Monitors. The first one should be there within an hour. Just hang on."

"Yes, sir," Don said. An hour. He was glad to know that. He didn't have much time in which to operate.

He let it go another five minutes, then he said, "Sir, they're increasing speed." He had flicked off the scanning of the Kraden. He couldn't afford to have them spot any of the damage, though that was unlikely at this angle.

"Damn," the admiral said, then rapidly fired some more into his other screens, barking one order after another.

Don said, letting his voice go very flat, "I'm going in, sir. They're putting on speed. In another five minutes they'll be underway to the point where I won't be able to follow, and neither will anybody else. They'll get completely clear, and the Almighty

Ultimate only knows where they're headed. Possibly to hit Earth itself."

The admiral looked up, startled. The commodore's eyes widened.

The admiral rasped, "Don't be a fool."

"They'll get away, sir," Don said, trying to make his face look determined. Knowing that the others could see his every motion, Don Mathers hit the cocking handle of his flakflak gun with the heel of his right hand.

The admiral snapped, "Let it go, you ass. You wouldn't last a second." Then, his voice higher, "That's an order, Lieutenant!"

"Yes, sir," Don Mathers said.

He flicked off his screen and grimaced sourly. He took up his vacuum bottle and finished the contents, then descended on the Kraden ship, his flakflak gun beaming it. He was going to have to expend every erg of energy in his One Man Scout to burn the other ship to the point where his attack would look authentic, and to eliminate all signs of previous action.

He swept it from prow to stern, taking particular care to fire all over the area where the extraterrestrial spaceship had taken its original hits. He raked it up and down until it was little more than a molten hulk.

And then, his offensive powers exhausted, he snapped his communications back on. The face of the commodore of the first squadron of his supposed reinforcements faded onto his screen.

The other, his face young, considering his rank, snapped, "Commodore Franco, Officer Commanding Task Force Three. How do things stand, Lieutenant? Is he still under observation?"

Don said, calmly, clearly, "Yes, sir. I think I've finished him, but perhaps you'd better approach with care."

"You've what!"

"Yes, sir."

VI

Don Mathers wasn't acquainted with the Lindbergh story. Had he been he could have been aware of the similarities to his landing at the space base and Lindbergh's coming down in Paris. Not only were all personnel of the base on hand, but the population of Center City and a dozen other nearby communities had erupted to greet him.

He was taken aback by the magnitude of the mob and a little apprehensive about setting down. There seemed to be police, or, more likely, soldiers, shoulder to shoulder to hold back the crowd so that it couldn't swarm out over the runway. If they broke through the cordon the fat was going to be in the fire. The V-102 had no power usable here within the atmosphere. He had to glide in to a landing. If the mob of cheering citizens broke through to the runway, he'd plow into them.

But the ranks of soldiers held and he came in, making a perfect landing and winding up before the hanger in which the V-102 was usually sheltered.

Before the hanger stood Sergeant Jerry Wilkins

and the rest of the mechanic crew. All were in dress uniform, rather than dirty coveralls and all were standing to attention. For once, the sergeant was minus the cynical expression on his wizened face.

Don Mathers, casting a somewhat apprehensive look at the cheering mob, climbed out and approached his crew.

He said to the sergeant, "You were right, Wilkins, the V-102 was tuned like a chronometer. It operated perfectly. Thanks. If even the slightest thing had gone wrong, I wouldn't be here and whatever that Kraden's mission was it probably would have been accomplished."

"Thank you, sir," Wilkins said.

A group of highly uniformed, highly bemedaled older officers was approaching.

Don grinned wryly at his crew and said, "Here comes the brass. Well, boys, take good care of the V-102. I'll be seeing you."

"Afraid the V-102 is out of our hands, sir," the sergeant told him. "The Space Academy and the Smithsonian Institution are fighting for her. Both want to enshrine her."

Inwardly, Don thought, "Almighty Ultimate!" He turned and faced the advancing brass. The only one he recognized was Commodore Bernklau and he was the lowest ranking officer among them.

Don came to the salute.

The five star Space Fleet admiral said, "At ease, Lieutenant, and, obviously, congratulations."

"Thank you, sir," Don said crisply.

The commodore said, "The news people would like to get to you, Donal, but orders are to avoid them until you have made your first report to the Octagon. I am to accompany you to Bost-Wash."

Don said, looking out at the cheering mob, and then down at his coveralls, "Yes, sir. But how do we get through that crowd to where I can change into uniform?"

One of the generals laughed and said, "We've foxed them, Lieutenant. The Presidential Jet has been sent to pick you up. It is equipped with uniforms of your size, and anything else you might need."

One of the fleet admirals grinned and said, "Including an autobar. I suspect you could use a drink after what you've been through."

"Yes, sir, I sure could, sir," Don said.

They all shook hands with him before moving along to the Presidential Jet.

"So long, sir," the sergeant called after him, unheard. He turned to the rest of the mechanics. "We'll never see him again," he said. "He's about to be, what's the word? deified. That means they make a god out of you."

Don Mathers had never been in Bost-Wash before, though he had flown over it. The city stretched from what had once been Boston to what had once been Washington. In fact, if anything, it would have been more accurate, these days, to call it Port-Port, since it was rapidly engulfing Portland, Maine, to the north, and Portsmouth, Virginia, to the south.

The Presidential Jet swooped in to the extensive landing field adjacent to the Octagon and Don Mathers, now in his sub-lieutenant's dress uniform, was hurried into a hover-limousine and into the bowels of the enormous military building.

The commodore explained. "We didn't let the word out that you were on your way here. We were afraid that a couple of million citizens might show up and not even the Octagon has the manpower on hand to hold back a crowd that big."

"Holy smokes," Don protested. "I didn't expect anything like this."

The commodore looked at him strangely. He said, "Donal, so far as we know, you are the only man ever to destroy a Kraden single-handed. In fact, your Miro Class cruiser is the first Kraden destroyed since the big shoot-out fifty years ago. Every human being alive has been wrapped up in this war for half a century and you're the first one to draw blood in all that time."

"Sheer luck," Don said.

"Of course. But nevertheless you did it."

They were whisked into a lavish conference room and Don was confronted by a dozen of the ranking military of the solar system.

He came to attention and saluted. None of them bothered to return it.

89

He said, "Sub-lieutenant Donal Mathers reporting."

His ultimate commander, Senior Admiral of the Space Forces Frol Rubinoff, said, "Relax, Donal. Have a seat. Would you like a drink?"

Don sat. He said, ruefully, "No, sir. I'd better not. I had a couple on the plane. I needed them then. But I guess I better not need any more now."

It wasn't that good a sally but all of them laughed, as though to put him at his ease.

They had a tape recorder before him but also all had scratch pads and stylos.

The Senior Admiral said, "Now, we want to get as much of this down as possible while it's still fresh in your mind. When did you first spot the Kraden?"

Don said, "He just suddenly materialized, sir. Bang, in front of me, only a few hundred kilometers off."

One of the others leaned forward and said, "So you think he emerged from hyper-space, as some have called it? That is, that the Kradens have accomplished faster than light travel?"

Don played it sincere. "I don't know, sir. All of a sudden, he was there."

To the extent he could, he stuck to the truth. Many of the questions they asked, he couldn't answer but seemingly did the best he could. In the heat of the action, he explained, a lot of details went by him.

One of them said, "Why in the world did you

switch off your scanners just at the point when you went into action? It would have been invaluable to have been able to watch the progress of the attack."

Don looked at him and said, "Yes, sir, but I had just been ordered by my fleet admiral not to attack. I was afraid that if I continued to communicate he would give me further orders that I felt I couldn't obey, not if the Kraden wasn't going to get away."

The Senior Admiral shook his head in rejection but also in admiration. He said, "You are a very undisciplined young man, Lieutenant. In this case, thank the Almighty Ultimate. What did you think you were going to accomplish going in to attack?"

"I . . . I'm not sure I know, sir. I guess that I thought that I might be able to divert him for a short time. Keep him busy until the Monitors came up. I wasn't as fast as he was by a long shot, but I was more maneuverable at short range. I . . . I didn't expect to be able to do much more than a mosquito could to an elephant."

One of the others shook his head. "You shouldn't have been able to," he muttered.

"Yes, sir," Don said.

The screen before the Senior Admiral lit up and he glowered at it impatiently. He growled, "I thought I had given orders that we were not to be disturbed under any circumstances."

But then he brought his eyes up and said, "The lieutenant has been taken out of our hands." He looked at Don. "The President of the Solar System League has ordered that you immediately be flown to New Geneva."

"Yes, sir," Don said, coming to his feet. It was a relief, though he tried not to let that show in his face. These were not stupid men. It might have been only a matter of time before one of them asked some question that he couldn't answer. Some question that would trip him up.

The Senior Admiral looked at the commodore and said, "Bernklau, see sub-lieutenant Mathers back to the Presidential Jet. It will not be necessary that you further accompany him."

"Yes, sir," the commodore said.

The Senior Admiral came back to Don. He said, "Sub-lieutenant Mathers, I congratulate you. You have conducted yourself in such manner that the whole human race can only be proud of you."

"Thank you, sir," Don said. He snapped the other a salute.

"It is I who should be saluting you," the older man said, returning the courtesy.

Don Mathers had never before been in Switzerland. The aircraft swooped into the landing field near Lake Leman on the outskirts of New Geneva with precision, the precision to be expected of the pilots of the Presidential Jet. There was only a small group, not all uniformed, to greet the new celebrity. Evidently, his movements were still being concealed.

Don Mathers went through the standard amenities, failing to remember the name of a single one of the committee. This was piling up so fast that his thinking was in a continuous state of turmoil.

Three limousines sped up and he was ushered into the middle one. There were two uniformed, stolid-faced chauffeurs in the front. Only one of the welcoming delegation got into the back with him, an elderly man in formal morning clothes and with a red ribbon across his chest. Don had forgotten his name but obviously he was some high ranking mucky-muck.

The caravan took off and the other told Don, "We have reserved a suite for you at the *Intercontinental*. It is conveniently located near the Palais des Nations."

Don knew what the Palais des Nations was. It was the parliament building of the Solar System League. First begun in 1929 for the League of Nations, later it had been taken over as the European Office of the United Nations Organization, and, after the coming of the Kradens and the institution of system-wide government, by the Solar System League. It was here that the president presided over the parliament, consisting of representatives from formerly sovereign nations on Earth and from all of the colonies.

As they progressed, his companion gave Don Mathers a running commentary, and it sounded as though he had been through it before, and much more than once. "This is the Rue de la Servette. If we continued along it we would pass through the Place des 22 Cantons, cross the Rhone river and be in the oldest part of the city. It is quite attractive. Geneva was originally settled by the Romans but most of its older buildings today are medieval."

Don, a product of modern North America, couldn't have cared less.

The city was a far cry from those he was used to in North America. There were no hi-rises, no modern buildings at all for all practical purposes. There was little in the way of advertising and traffic seemed strangely slow, and even sparse. The pedestrians strolled, rather than walking briskly. Some of the side streets were winding and, of all things, cobbled.

The caravan turned left and they drove up to a side entry of a large, ultra-deluxe hotel. Doors were flung open by chauffeurs and the whole party hustled inside.

"You are being kept incognito until tomorrow," his formally-clad guide told him.

"What happens tomorrow?" Don said.

They were heading for an elevator bank in a wing of the hotel, avoiding entering the lobby.

"You are to be presented to the Parliament of the Solar System League, or, at least to those elements of it that have had the time to arrive."

They zipped up to the eighteenth floor of the hotel and Don was ushered into his suite.

When his guide had told him that they had reserved a suite for him, he had meant a *suite*. Other than the quarters of Lawrence Demming in Center City, Don had never seen anything like this.

His guide told him, "And this is Pierre, your majordomo."

Pierre bowed slightly from the hips. He looked and dressed like a head waiter, Don decided. "At your service, sir," he said in impeccable English.

The whole delegation had entered the suite and now stood in a group. Don wondered what the hell they were supposed to be doing. Thus far, aside from the handshakes and murmured greetings at the airport, they had accomplished nothing. He had a sneaking suspicion that the same group met all arriving VIPs. And did exactly what they were doing now. Nothing.

His guide, or whatever the hell he was, said, "And now, Lieutenant Mathers, it is to be assumed that you are fatigued and certainly need rest for tomorrow. I would suggest that you take your meals here in your suite, rather than enter the public dining room, where you might be recognized. The chef will make every effort to excel himself in your behalf. He has been let in on the secret of your indentity. His specialty is *pieds de porc au madere*."

"Well . . . thanks," Don said.

The delegation bowed themselves out.

Don tossed his hat to a side table and said to the flunky, "How about a drink?"

"Certainly, Monsieur." The majordomo clapped his hands and a waiter materialized.

Don sunk down into a chair and eased his shoes off. The Presidential Jet had been stocked with a supply of uniforms and other clothing in anticipation of his needs, but they had slipped up on the shoes, which were a bit too tight.

"What do you drink around here?" he said.

"Monsieur, since the vineyards have been turned over to producing cereals, new wine vintages are no longer with us. However, the former manager of the *Intercontinental* was farsighted enough to lay down an extensive stock in the cellars. I can recommend a bottle of Silvaner."

"Whatever that is," Don said. "All right, we'll give it a try."

Pierre said to the waiter, "A bottle of well-chilled Silvaner, Hans."

The waiter disappeared.

Don said, "These damn shoes are too tight."

Pierre said quickly, "I shall have a representative from the hotel shop come up immediately to fit you, sir."

Don, in his stockinged feet, went over to the terrace and looked out over Lake Leman. It was a superlative view and as an attractive body of water as he had ever seen.

He said, "That's a beautiful castle over there."

Pierre said, "That is Chillon, Monsieur Mathers.

Immortalized by Lord Byron in his *Prisoner of Chillon.*"

Don had never heard of Lord Byron but didn't want to show himself up to the servant. Almighty Ultimate, this was living. He had eaten and drunk like a king on the Presidential Jet but he couldn't wait to get into the fleshpots of Geneva. This was living!

In the morning, they came for him, two Space Service colonels. By their insignia, both were commanders of Space Monitors.

Don didn't have his cap on, so he didn't salute. Not sure what this day held for him, he had refrained from getting even moderately drenched the night before and was now in good shape.

The first colonel said, snap in his voice, "The President of the Solar System League sends his compliments and requires that you attend an extraordinary session of the Parliament of the Solar System League."

"Yes, sir," Don said.

Pierre brought his hat.

They left formally, not speaking, eyes straight ahead.

This time Don Mathers was not shielded from the lobby. They marched out the front entry. There were four infantrymen there, all captains, but armed with laser rifles. They snapped to attention. Hotel guests and pedestrians stared. Don was still incognito. Geneva was used to VIPs but they didn't recognize this one in the uniform of a space sub-lieutenant.

They drove in silence to the Palais des Nations.

At the entry, there was an honor guard of spacemen. They presented arms, or snapped to salute, as Don and his two colonels entered.

He was marched up this corridor, down that, and finally wound up in an enormous auditorium. He was marched to the podium. There were six men there, five seated, one standing. The one standing was a Black. Don obviously knew who he was. He also knew three of the others. They were continuously on the news.

The two colonels saluted, wheeled and marched off.

The Tri-Di cameras were already fully operational.

Kwame Kumasi, this decade's President of the Solar System League, stepped forward. Don Mathers stood to rigid attention.

The President read the citation. It was short, as Galactic Medal of Honor citations always were.

". . . for conspicuous gallantry far and beyond the call of duty, in which you single-handedly and against unbelievably desperate odds attacked and destroyed an enemy cruiser while piloting a One Man Scout armed only with a short beam flakflak gun."

He pinned a small bit of metal and ribbon to Don Mathers' tunic. The Galactic Medal of Honor was possibly the most insignificant looking medal in the history of military decorations. It was a tiny cross of platinum, on a red ribbon, without inscription.

The president, his ebony face beaming, said, "Colonel Mathers, only twelve of these decorations have ever been awarded in human history before."

Don said, "*Sub-lieutenant* Mathers, Mr. President."

Kwame Kumasi smiled and said, "Donal Mathers, you are famed for the fact that you disobey the orders of even your highest ranking officers. However, as President of the Solar System League I am your ultimate commander-in-chief, and you must not contradict your commander-in-chief, *Colonel* Mathers."

The packed chamber reverberated with cheers and applause.

When it had died somewhat, Don Mathers said simply, "But I only did my duty."

It was a slogan that was to sweep the solar system. During the following months when anyone active in defense performed a task beyond the call of the expected, he or she invariably said, when commended, "But I only did my duty."

The President looked into the face of Don Mathers and said, "As President of the Solar System League, I hold the most prestigous position for a member of the human race to achieve. However, Colonel Mathers . . . I wish I was you."

At the time, it didn't occur to Don Mathers that he was the *thirteenth* man to be awarded the Galactic Medal of Honor—the bearer of which could do no wrong.

VII

The President, still beaming, had shaken hands and said, "And now, Colonel Mathers, it is to be assumed that you have relatives and friends who are most anxious for your company."

"Thank you, Mr. President," Don said. It was a dismissal. He did an about face and retraced the route the two colonels had brought him along earlier. The Tri-Di cameras followed him all the way to the door. The assembly was applauding again.

However, the President had been incorrect. Don had neither relatives nor friends waiting for him here—even in North America the nearest relatives he could think of were an aunt, somewhere out on the West Coast and two cousins of whom he had long since lost track.

Short though the time had been since he had first entered the auditorium of the Parliament building, there was already a crowd before the Palais des Nations, perhaps as many as a hundred persons. They applauded as he descended the steps. Some were obviously newspeople, complete with their complicated equipment, but the majority were evidently passersby who had heard the broadcast.

Some pressed closer, and for the first time in his life Don Mathers was asked for his autograph and then again and again. Others wanted to shake his hand, and shook. He rather desperately fielded questions from the media people.

No, he had no immediate plans other than to return to his base and to duty.

One of the reporters called, "Have hopes of getting another Kraden, Colonel?"

Don laughed ruefully.

Was he married?

"No."

"Did he have a fiancée?"

Don set his face. "There was a labor shortage in the new mining developments on Callisto. She signed up for a five year tour, feeling it her duty beyond personal affairs." It was a lie, but it sounded good. Dian had most definitely severed their relationship.

The crowd was getting bigger by the minute. Before he knew it he'd be in a mob big enough to crush him.

He held up his two arms. "Please," he said. "I have things I must do."

Somewhat to his surprise, they meekly pressed back and opened a way for him. When he hurried through, none followed. He had to admire their courtesy. In Center City autograph hunters and celebrity seekers were on the more aggressive side.

He made his way down the Avenue de France, in the direction of the lake, not knowing exactly what he had in mind, now that he was on the town.

He spotted an auto rental agency and entered. A clerk came up to him, blinked in sudden recognition, and said, "Just a minute, Colonel Mathers." He turned and sped off to return in moments with an older man, obviously one of the enterprise's top staff, if not the owner.

He said unctuously, "It is a pleasure to welcome you, Colonel Mathers."

Don said, "Look, I'd like to rent a car but the trouble is I don't have my driver's license. I left America quickly without being able to get hold of my papers."

The other smiled. "But you are Donal Mathers. You don't need a driver's license. You don't need any kind of a license, to do anything, Colonel."

That hadn't occurred to Don.

"What model appeals to you?" the other said, indicating a large selection with a sweep of his hand. Several of the employees had come around and stood back away goggling the hero.

He said, pointing out a very recent model sports number. "That's a beauty."

"The keys are in it, Colonel."

Don brought his Universal Credit Card from his uniform tunic. "Do I pay now? Or leave a deposit?"

"The car is yours, Colonel Mathers."

Don stared at him.

The other managed a short wry laugh. "Colonel, can you imagine the advertising value both to my business here and to the manufacturers of the vehicle? I am sure that they will insist on reimbursing me when it is announced that the first car selected by the bearer of the Galactic Medal of Honor was one of theirs."

That hadn't occurred to Don either.

He said, simply, "Thanks. But I won't be needing it long. I'll return it when I leave Geneva."

"Whatever you wish, Colonel. But you can take it back to America with you if you so desire."

Don Mathers, set back by his reception at the auto agency, turned right at the Rue de Lausanne and headed down toward the center of town. The little sports hovercar was a dream to drive manually. Come to think of it, the car didn't contain controls for automated driving. Evidently, this city hadn't automated its streets. He was surprised; as capital of the Solar System League the town was one of the most important on Earth.

He drove around a bit through the medieval parts of Geneva, until something came to him. He had no wrist chronometer. That too had been left in his locker at the base when he had substituted coveralls for uniform preparatory to take off in his patrol. He could, of course, have dialed the hour on his new transceiver, which he had picked up on the plane along with fresh uniforms, but it was more time consuming than a wrist chronometer.

The city was full of chronometer shops. He pulled up before a rather large one, and emerged from the car. There was a sidewalk cafe next to the shop, most of the tables taken. Someone spotted him and came to his feet and began to applaud. Others looked up in puzzlement, also recognized Don Mathers, and came to their feet and clapped their hands.

Don hurried into the shop. He'd be in another circle of autograph hunters, if he didn't look out.

Inside the shop, a girl clerk looked up. Her eyes widened.

Don said, "I need a wrist chronometer." The next came out automatically. "Not too expensive a one."

Her hand trembling, she indicated showcase after showcase of instruments. She said, her voice trembling as well, "We handle Patek-Philippe, Vacheron-Constantin, Audermars-Piguet and Piaget."

By this time, every clerk and customer in the extensive shop were staring at him, to his discomfort.

He pointed out one of the chronometers, a Piaget. "How much is that one?"

She shook her head in confusion. She was a little tyke, about twenty-five, Don estimated, and with that overly-scrubbed appearance that only the Swiss seem to maintain.

She said, "There is no price. The manager would never forgive me if I charged you for one of our products. Neither would the Piaget Company."

"Certainly not," a voice from behind them said indignantly. The newcomer wore formal morning clothing and had a carnation in his lapel. He had in one hand a sheet of heavy white paper and in the other a stylo. The paper bore the store's name in elaborate engraving. He said, "Colonel Mathers, I saw the broadcast—as did everyone else, I suppose —of you being awarded the Galactic Medal of Honor. Would it be possible to secure your signature? I would like to frame it and display it in this room."

"Why, of course," Don said, taking the stationery and putting it down on the showcase, the better to sign it. He wrote, *Sub-lieutenant Donal Mathers.*

When he looked up the Piaget was on the counter.

The shop manager smiled and said, "You have forgotten. It's *Colonel* Mathers now. I am surprised that Kwame Kumasi didn't make you a general."

"I don't know how to be a general," Don said gruffly, and handing back the paper. "I'm not sure that I know how to be a colonel."

He took up the chronometer and put it on his wrist. "Thanks," he said and hurried out when he noticed that others in the store were beginning to close in on him.

He climbed back into the car and took off. The

new chronometer revealed that it was lunch time. He had noted a restaurant as he drove down the Rue de Lausanne earlier, located right on the side of the lake. He headed back for it.

He parked in the lot and headed for the park with its outside tables. The panorama was wonderful. A maitre d' sped up, flanked by two captains.

"Colonel Mathers," the leader burbled delightedly, "what an honor that you have chosen *La Perle du Lac* in which to lunch."

"Yeah," Don said. "Is it possible for me to get a table off aways so that I won't be bothered?"

"But certainly, Colonel." The other led the way.

There was a small orchestra that was playing a currently popular air. They suddenly broke it off and went into the *Interplanetary Anthem*. Various of the diners looked up from conversation and food and spotted Don. There was a standing ovation. He nodded and smiled in embarrassment and hurried on to his remote table. This was beginning to wear on him a little.

After the meal, a fantastic production with several wines, Don finished his liqueur and asked the maitre d' for his bill, even as he reached for his Universal Credit Card. All during the lunch the maitre d' had hovered nearby. So did two waiters. He noticed them fending off other diners who from time to time tried to come over to him, menus and stylos in hand, obviously autograph hunting. He pretended not to see them.

The headwaiter smiled. "Colonel, I am afraid that your money is of no value in *La Perle du Lac*, not just for this luncheon but whenever you honor us." He paused and added, "In fact, Colonel Mathers, I doubt if there is a restaurant in the solar system where your money holds value. Or that there ever will be."

Don Mathers was taken aback all over again. He was only beginning to realize the ramifications of his Galactic Medal of Honor. He had entered his partnership with Demming and Rostoff with the expectation of becoming rich beyond dreams of avarice and he had some pretty avaricious dreams. But what use was it to be rich if you couldn't spend your money?

Lunch over, he returned to the hotel to take a siesta. He had eaten and drank too much. He was going to have to watch this. He was a good trencherman but if he let himself go the way he had been doing lately he was going to wind up as pig-like as Demming.

He made the mistake of entering the *Intercontinental* through the main lobby and was immediately swarmed upon by news media people, hotel employees and guests. In fact, he suspected that some of them weren't even guests but had come in off the streets to catch a glimpse of him. He was beginning to wonder how Tri-Di stars, top politicians, and other celebrities stood it, day in, day out.

He finally made his way through and to the elevators. At least they didn't crowd in after him. He said into the order screen, "18th Floor."

"Yes, Colonel Mathers," the mechanical voice said.

He wondered if the hotel computer knew the face and name of all of the guests. He had never been in a hotel this luxurious before.

The identity screen of his suite picked him up upon his approach and the door swung open.

Only a couple of yards beyond was Pierre, his majordomo. Had the man been standing there, awaiting him, all this time? It was more likely, he decided, that one of the reception clerks had phoned up to alert the servant.

Don tossed his hat to one side and said peevishly, "Listen, Pierre, I want some civilian clothes. Everybody recognizes me in this uniform. I'm evidently a seven-day wonder."

Pierre said, with his little bow, "Of course, Monsieur. But I rather doubt, Colonel Mathers, that the wonder will be over in seven days. After all, you are the only man in the system to hold your decoration. I shall send to the men's shop for tailors."

Don said, not as graciously as he might have, "I haven't the time to have something tailored. I'll be wanting to go out tonight."

"I am sure that they will be able to cooperate, Monsieur. I'll summon them immediately."

"Do that," Don said. "I'd like to get it over with and take a nap."

The tailors came and went and Don took to his bed in the suite's master bedroom. He wondered who was handling the bill for a suite this far out. What in the hell did he need with all these rooms? The place was big enough to hold not just a party, but a ball. Probably the government was picking up the tab, he decided; after all, they'd brought him here.

It was dark by the time he revived. He got up and stretched and immediately came a gentle knock at the door.

"Come in," he growled, running his tongue over his teeth. His mouth tasted like hell. He'd been drinking too much, eating too much.

One of the servants entered. He said, "Good evening, sir. I am James, your valet."

Don took him in. He looked like a damn queer. Don said, "I don't need a valet. I can dress myself."

"Yes, sir. Your suits have arrived, sir. And your haberdashery."

"All right, bring them in."

James left and returned shortly bearing a considerable load of clothing. He was followed by two more servants, each weighted down. They made three trips, in all. The room's closets and drawers were just barely sufficient to house it. Included were some colonel's rank uniforms.

Don took it all in. "Almighty Ultimate," he said, shaking his head. Seemingly, it was enough clothing to last him for the rest of his life. He looked at James. "Find me something to go out in tonight. Something inconspicuous."

"Yes, sir." James marched to a closet. The other two servants bowed themselves out.

"How big's the, uh, staff here?" Don said.

"There are six of us, sir, including Monsieur Pierre. Of course, if the Colonel wished to entertain, additional assistance would be immediately available." The valet deftly selected clothing and laid it out on the bed.

"I think I can skimp by on six," Don said. "Get Pierre, I want to ask him something."

· "Yes, sir.".

Pierre appeared promptly.

Don told him, "I'll be going out tonight. What are the best nightclubs in town?"

The other said judiciously, "I should say, Colonel Mathers, that the liveliest is the *Ba-Ta-Clan*. The *Moulin Rouge* is also very chic and is reputed to have a very good floorshow. Then there is the *Chez Maxim's*, about the same. The *Pussy Cat Saloon* is said to be quite hilarious."

"I'm not feeling particularly hilarious," Don said. "Which of them has the dimmest atmosphere?"

"I would say the *Moulin Rouge*, Mon Colonel."

"All right, get me a drink. I'm dying on the vine. Make it spirits, whiskey or cognac, with soda."

The drink came before he was finished bathing and dressing. It was the best Scotch he had ever tasted, and certainly not the ersatz which was the common thing these days. Barley was no longer used for the distilling of spirits.

"Where'd this come from?" he said, surprised.

"The President himself sent over a case from his private cellars," Pierre said.

"A case!" Don said. "What does he expect me to do, take a bath in it?"

"That is only the whiskey, sir. He dispatched other beverages as well."

Don finished off his dressing. "All right, now, how can I get out of this hotel without that mob of gawkers spotting me?"

Pierre told him.

"And what's the address of this *Moulin Rouge* and how do I get to it? I don't want to be stopping to ask for directions. That ceremony took place a few hours ago, and it was kept secret until the very last, but I've got a sneaking suspicion that by now every newsman in Europe is on his way to Geneva."

"Just a moment, sir." The other left, to return in no time at all with a map of Geneva, which he spread out on a small table. "The *Moulin Rouge* is located at 1 Avenue du Mail." He brought forth a stylo and marked it, and then quickly made several other crosses and wrote above each one. "And these are the other night spots I mentioned, Colonel."

He folded the map and handed it over.

VIII

Getting out of the *Intercontinental* undetected was simplicity itself. Evidently, Don Mathers wasn't the first reluctant celebrity to desire a rear exit. One of the servants had been sent down to get his sports hovercar and bring it around to the small door off what amounted to an alley in the hotel's rear. There had been a semi-private elevator to utilize and then a short, empty hall to navigate to the exit.

He brought forth his map, checked it, then put it, opened, on the seat beside him. No problem at all.

Only one thing came up on his way to the night-spot. He pulled off some traffic violation, the nature of which he never did understand, not being used to local laws, and was stopped immediately by an officious-looking traffic policeman in the green uniform and stiff leather helmet of the Geneva police.

The cop began to blurt something at him in German and then, when Don looked blank, in French.

Don said finally, in English, "Look, I'm sorry, I'm not acquainted with local laws. I'm Colonel Mathers, and . . ."

The police officer's mouth clicked shut and he stepped back and sprang to attention and saluted. But then he stepped forward again, his hand dragging a notebook from his pocket. "Colonel," he said, "I wonder if I could have your autograph. My younger son collects. He would give his arm for your signature."

Wearily, Don took the proffered stylo and signed the notebook. He remembered to make it *Colonel* Donal Mathers this time. Obviously, he was free to go. He went.

The *Moulin Rouge* was by far the most elaborate nightclub that Don had ever experienced. He had never been in the income bracket to afford much in the way of nightlife.

He was surprised at the number of employees. Back in Center City almost everything in the way of services was automated, computerized, and sterile, and such things as live waiters were frowned upon on the theory that they should be working in some branch of the defense effort. As it was, a parking attendant took his car off and Don headed for the entrance which was presided over by two doormen, both dressed in uniforms as elaborate as that of a Rumanian Rear Admiral.

They opened up snappily and he advanced to be met by a gushing headwaiter.

"Colonel Mathers! A pleasure to greet you tonight. Your reserved table is awaiting you." He was flanked by three waiters, much as the maitre d' had been at the restaurant that afternoon. Why in the hell should he need four waiters, in all?

Don frowned at the other and said, "How did you know I was coming?"

"Your hotel phoned, Colonel."

That must have been Pierre. Nobody else knew that he was on his way. Not unless his suite was bugged, which seemed unlikely.

The bowing, smiling headwaiter said, "However, we had a table reserved for you already, Colonel, on the off chance that you might grace us with your presence. I suspect that every other club in town has done likewise. If you will please follow."

When they entered the main room an orchestra was playing for a floor show dance team. In the middle of an intricate step, it suddenly broke off and swung into the stirring *Interplanetary Anthem*. The startled dancers were lucky that one of them didn't fall and break a leg.

The some two hundred celebrants in the *Moulin Rouge* rose to a man—and woman—and clapped their hands as he followed the headwaiter across the floor. His damned civilian clothes weren't doing a thing for him, so far as disguising his identity was concerned.

However, prices at the *Moulin Rouge* seemingly eliminated all but cultivated, upper class clientele. When Don had been seated, they all resumed their own places, and except for covert glances from time to time, he was left to himself. No handshakers or autograph seekers here.

The table was a good one but discreetly located. The floorshow resumed.

There was an ice bucket to one side. The headwaiter brought a bottle half out of it. "I took the liberty, Colonel, of chilling a bottle. It is Vintage Mumms and from the owner's own stock."

"Vintage Mumms?" Don said. "You mean champagne?" He had never tasted real champagne.

"Yes, Colonel Mathers. I understand that there are but few bottles remaining in the world. It is a shame. When I was a boy it was highly preferred. However, if you do not desire a sparkling wine——"

"Oh, no. No, no," Don said hurriedly. "I'll be glad to try it."

The maitre d' was taking care of him personally, though two of his assistants hovered in the background. He expertly flicked out the cork, wrapped the very chilled bottle in a napkin, poured half a glass and looked hopefully expectant.

Don had seen Lawrence Demming go through the routine. He took up the champagne glass and took a small sip. It was the best drink he could remember ever having tasted.

He nodded and said, "Excellent." The other beamed satisfaction and filled the glass three quarters full.

The headwaiter said, "Is there anything else, sir?

Have you dined. Our head chef is impatient——"

"No . . . not yet," Don told him. The whole atmosphere was exciting and he loved it. This was the life Demming and Rostoff had hinted at.

Or anything else?" the headwaiter urged.

Don said ruefully, "Perhaps some companionship. I am afraid I know nobody in Geneva except . . . the President of the Solar System League and some of his aides."

"Feminine companionship, Colonel?"

Don followed along. "I am very fond of the ladies." He thought, good grief, does a place as swank as this have a selection of whores?

The other made a slight gesture. "Do any of the ladies present attract you?"

Don still followed along with what he assumed was supposed to be a joke. He said, "Almost all of them. I have never seen such an assemblage of attractive women. Unfortunately——"

"Who do you think particularly attractive, Colonel Mathers? The headwaiter refilled his glass, though it was but half empty.

Don smiled and considered the selection of some one hundred women. He assumed that the headwaiter would produce a professional as near the original as possible. He said finally, "That redheaded girl over there, in the white evening gown. I don't believe I've ever seen a more attractive young woman, even on Tri-Di shows and, the Almighty

Ultimate knows, on Tri-Di, even if they don't start glamorous, the pro beauticians can make them so."

"A moment, Colonel."

Don stared after him, in puzzlement, as the headwaiter took off across the room. He stopped at the table where the redhead was seated with a distinguished companion, bent and spoke in low tone to them. For a moment, the man stiffened. The girl shot a quick glance over at Don, then looked away.

The headwaiter had stepped back several discreet feet. The girl whispered something to her escort, who said something in return.

She came to her feet and the headwaiter led her to Don's table, to his absolute and utter surprise. He shot to his feet.

The headwaiter said, "It is obviously not necessary to introduce Colonel Donal Mathers. Colonel, this is the Gräffin Greta von Emden und Garmisch."

She was looking at him starry-eyed.

Behind her, her escort had stood, and now, very Prussian, he clicked his heels, bowed to Don, turned and strode from the room, looking only straight ahead.

She was quite the most striking girl Don could ever remember having seen. Girl was the term, since she looked considerably younger than she had when seated across the room. She couldn't have been more than in her early twenties. Her red hair was a dark red and piled atop her head, in a style of years before. Her delicate ears would have inspired a poet.

Her complexion was of the light fineness that only the northern races seem to be able to achieve. Her nose was slightly thin and aristocratic; her mouth delicate, though full-lipped and red. Don had not failed to notice the perfection of her figure as she crossed the dance floor. It seemed more mature than one of her years would ordinarily have boasted.

The waiters scurried up and held the chairs for Don and the newcomer.

The headwaiter had magically produced a second glass and now poured wine for her, returned the bottle to the ice bucket and made off. The waiters also faded back.

Don was flustered and said, "I hope that your boyfriend wasn't——"

Her voice went with face and figure, sweet but with a slight trill in it. She shook her head. "But he is not my boyfriend, he is my husband." Her English was excellent. Seemingly, everyone in Geneva spoke the language.

That stopped him for a moment, but then he thought he understood and said, "Oh, I see. You have a friendly arrangement. Both of you are free to go your own way."

She opened her gray-green eyes wide. "Oh, no. Our marriage is a happy one. You see, we are on our honeymoon."

He bug-eyed her and couldn't think of anything to say.

She said, and her voice was very slight now, and

her eyes down, looking into her champagne which she hadn't tasted as yet, "You see, we both watched, on the Tri-Di, the presentation ceremony this morning. We both cried, although, in spite of the fact that I have known him for years, I have never seen Kurt cry before. Possibly you weren't aware of the fact that it was all recorded, all taken down on video-tape by the fleet admiral, and it was all replayed on the Tri-Di, all over the world, all over the Solar System. You disobeyed orders. You said, 'I'm going in,' and you banged the cocking hammer, I think that is what my husband named it, of your flak-flak gun, or whatever they call it. And some of the commentators say your chances were one in a thousand of surviving at all, not to speak of destroying the monsters."

Don's lips were dry. He took a desperate sip of his champagne. She was right, he hadn't known that the whole thing had been video-taped.

She went on, "Later when the Space Monitors of our fleet came up, eight of them, their commodore continued to video-tape it all. The ruined Miro Class cruiser—I think they called it—that great, hulking spacecraft of the Kradens. And, for a moment, he caught your tiny One Man Scout, flying past its bulk. We have many myths and legends in my country, Colonel Mathers, about knights and princes fighting dragons, but never such a small knight against such a large dragon."

Don said, "What has this got to do with your husband leaving you here with me?"

Greta said simply, "My husband is honored."

By this time she had sipped at her wine and smiled at him over the glass. "As I am, to be chosen to be your companion the very evening of the day you won your award."

A waiter scurried up and refilled their glasses, held the bottle up, saw it was nearly empty, and scurried off with it.

For a moment, Don felt the first twinge within him since he had made his decision in the One Man Scout and went on in quest of glory and wealth. He put the feeling down. Demming and Rostoff had been right. It was a dog-eat-dog system, each man out for himself. Take what you can get. If you don't, somebody else will.

The waiter came back with more wine, put it into the ice bucket and swirled it around.

Don invited her to dance and, as to be expected, she was perfect, as her face and figure were perfect. You did not breed such women, save in time, centuries of time.

He said, "What is a Gräffin?"

She smiled up at him and said, "In actuality, there is no such thing any more. Some of we who were of the aristocracy, a century and a half ago, still use our titles but they are meaningless. A gräffin is the German equivalent of a French countess. The equivalent of being the wife of an earl, in England. My husband is a Graf."

"I see," Don said. "So, if the, ah, Kaiser was ever brought back to Germany, you would again be a countess."

She smiled again. "It seems unlikely."

As they danced, the other couples made room for them, so that it was as though they were in the center of a circle, which made Don uncomfortable. Something else made him additionally uncomfortable. They would pass the empty table where Greta and her husband had been seated—enjoying their honeymoon.

He said, suddenly, "What do you say we get out of here and go somewhere else?"

As always, there was no bill.

They stopped, in turn, at the various nightspots that Pierre had recommended, breaking the routine of drinking somewhat at the *Ba-Ta-Clan* where they ate. But even there, the food was taken with wine —once again from the private cellars of the manager, and not usually for sale. Don was too far gone by this time to appreciate it.

The fog rolled in somewhere along there and when it rolled out again, it was to find that he and Greta had acquired friends, two Space Service officers in the uniform of captains, and their girls. Nobody was feeling pain. They were in the *Pussy Cat Saloon* and had evidently been there for some time.

The captains, deferential to Don, in spite of them

all being drenched, didn't discuss his feat against the Kraden, nor his decoration. Possibly that had come sooner while he was in the alcoholic fog, or possibly they thought it would be bad manners, bad taste. It was all very hilarious.

And at the other tables, no matter how loud his party was being, the other club-goers were smiling, looking over at the new hero sympathetically. Obviously, they thought he had every right to be intoxicated on this, of all nights.

Greta was looking at him a little worriedly. She herself had taken far less than any of the others, by the looks of her.

Finally, she whispered to him, "It's getting very late. Shall we have a last drink in . . . your suite, or mine?"

He looked at her blankly, woozily. "Your suite? But, well, your husband. . . ."

She cast her eyes down, a characteristic gesture of hers and said in a small voice, "I am sure that my husband is discreet. He will not be there."

He shook his head in continued amazement at this whole situation. He said, his voice slurring slightly, "Perhaps it had better be your place. There are so many media people, autograph hunters and so forth besieging my hotel that they'd surely spot us and your name would be linked to mine, epecially if you and your husband are as well known as I suspect you are."

"Very well," she said, taking up her bag.

They said their goodbyes to the rest of the party, as quickly as they could get away. As usual, there was no bill.

Her hotel was the *Des Bergues* on the Quai des Bergues, opposite the Rousseau Islands. It was far smaller than the *Intercontinental* but had a distinguished atmosphere, and one that dripped expensiveness. The Graf and his Gräffin were obviously not exactly poverty-stricken.

They hurried through the lobby and, for once, Don got the impression that he hadn't been recognized. Greta took him to a terrace suite on one of the upper floors.

She looked at him quizzically and said, "Are you sure that you want another drink?"

He sank into a chair and grinned at her and shook his head. "No, not at all sure."

She seemed relieved at that and said, "Just a moment and I'll be with you . . . Don."

The drive over in the open sports car had revived him considerably, but he was still far from being cold sober.

When she reentered, she was in a black negligee, and barefooted. The negligee looked as though it had cost a few months of Don's pay—if not more.

Her eyes were down, demurely.

He couldn't take his eyes from her, sweeping her from head to foot and back. The nightgown was translucent, if not actually transparent.

When he had surfeited himself, and was stretched out on his back, breathing deeply, she spoke for the first time, her voice low, as it usually was when she spoke to him. "Did I make you happy?"

"Yes," he murmured. What else could he say?

She said, so softly he could hardly make it out, "Am I the first woman you have had since your return from destroying the monsters?"

"Yes."

She sighed, before falling into sleep, "I shall have something to tell my grandchildren."

IX

Colonel Donal Mathers returned to North America on a Space Service supersonic jet. He could have made it considerably quicker on one of the rocket shuttle craft, but he was in no hurry. He had gotten in with four or five fleet admirals and commodores and they continued the bust, which had started in Paris, all the way to Bost-Wash.

The past eight or ten days—Don had lost count —had been one long prolonged lost weekend. It had begun, of course, there in Geneva but then, one morning, he had awakened in the *Nouveau Ritz* in Paris. The new Ritz was situated in the same location as the old, on the Place Vendôme, and Napoleon the First still graced the top of the pillar in the square's center. Not that Don would have known; he had never been in Paris before.

When he awakened that day—it couldn't be called morning—it was to shakily reach out for the bottle of Anti-Alc which he had taken to leaving on the bedside table. He shook out two of them—it took two these days, rather than the prescribed one —and looked for a carafe of water. There wasn't any. Muttering profanity, he got up and staggered to the bathroom. There was drinking water there, of course, and he shakily poured a glass and washed down his two pills.

Still feeling like death, he wavered into the bathroom and to one of the windows. It overlooked the Place Vendôme, which he didn't recognize, not even recalling ever having seen pictures of it. He thought that possibly he was somewhere in Italy.

Anti-Alc is quick-acting. It had to be. It was customarily taken when the patient felt he was on the verge of hangover oblivion.

The furniture of the living room was Louis the Fourteenth. Not that Don knew, or cared. It looked ornately uncomfortable to him. Something like Lawrence Demming's Swiss chalet penthouse, on top of the Interplanetary Lines Building in Center City. A damn museum setting.

He made his way over to the desk and was gratified to find a modern TV phone screen there.

He flicked it on and when the face of a very polite young man appeared, said, "Where in the hell am I?"

The other blinked and hesitated a moment before answering in complete detail. "You are in the Royal Suite of the Nouveau Ritz Hotel, in the City of Paris, in the area which was once known as France, in Europe, mon Colonel."

Don Mathers closed his eyes, the hangover not quite completely killed. "Oh, I am, eh?"

"Oui, mon Colonel."

"Speak English, dammit," Don growled, though what the other had said was obviously quite clear.

"Yes, Colonel Mathers. Is there some manner in which I could serve you?"

"Yeah. Send up a lot of breakfast. Oh, just a minute. Is there an autobar in this damn suite?"

"Yes, Colonel Mathers. It is disguised in the, ah, buffet to your immediate right."

Don flicked off the screen and went over to the buffet. Sure enough, part of the top lifted to reveal an elaborate autobar. He dialed a Bloody Mary, with a double shot of vodka, and stood there, still a bit shakily, until the bottom of the delivery area sank to return with the drink. He took it up and returned to the window to stare out.

So this was Paris. All his life he had wanted to see Paris.

But what had been his immediate idea of coming here? He couldn't remember. The last thing he could recall, with any clarity at all, was a fantastic party. He couldn't even remember who had thrown it. There had been a lot of media people there, but as fellow guests, rather than at work. There had been some fellow Space Service officers, of higher ranks, and, oh yes, there had been several celebrities from the entertainment world. One in particular, the reigning sex symbol of the Tri-Di musical comedies these days.

He closed his eyes and shook his head in an effort to achieve clearer memory. As he recalled, she wasn't nearly as beautifully sexy in person as she was on lens. However, he couldn't waste the opportunity. He had spent some time in bed with her. During the party, or after? He was damned if he could remember.

But why in the hell had he come to Paris, and, for that matter, how had he gotten here? The first part of the question finally came to him, but he never did find out the second.

When he had ordered a lot of breakfast, they had taken him at his word. None of this Continental breakfast nonsense, croissants and butter and marmalade and coffee. They brought him every type of breakfast known in the West—and some items from the Orient, for all he knew. Ham, bacon and sausage, all of various types. Eggs a half dozen ways. Cereals. Various types of toast and muffins. Kidneys, kippers and finnan haddie, British style. Caviar, smoked sturgeon and salmon and other *Zukouski*, Russian style. Cheeses and cold meats, Dutch style. Herring on ice with chives and sour cream sauce, smoked eel and smoked reindeer tongues, Scandinavian style. It had taken three waiters, accompanied by a captain, to wheel it all in.

What the hell did they think he was, a squadron?

The waiters hovered about, but he dismissed them, after giving the captain an autograph. He went on back to the autobar and, in view of the fact that he had finished the Bloody Mary, dialed an ice cold double aquavit. He put that down and returned to the food.

Long since, in his drinking career, he had learned to get plenty of food into his stomach before going into the next day of a binge. And he had every intention of continuing this particular binge.

By the time he had finished breakfast, the day was waning.

He went on back into the bedroom in which he had slept—he was to find later that there were three bedrooms in the Royal Suite—and looked around. His clothes were strewn about on the floor. He had been wearing one of his colonel's uniforms.

The hell with that. He went back to the living room and to the phone screen, called the desk and told them he wanted some clothes. The obsequious sycophant on the screen gushingly assured him that representatives of the men's shop would be up immediately.

After he had flicked off the screen, he looked at it for a moment and wondered what would happen if somewhere along here someone actually presented him with a bill. He doubted if he had enough credits in the data banks to pay for a fraction of the tab he was running up in this place.

Hell, they could sue him. That'd be a laugh. How could you sue a holder of the Galactic Medal of Honor? He was getting used to just what that meant.

Eventually bathed, shaved and dressed, he got himself another drink and with it went over to the window and stared out again. It was dark. Why in the hell had he come to Paris?

And then it came back to him.

That conversation he'd had with Harry Amanroder, proprietor of the Nuevo Mexico Bar. The discussion about Colin Casey.

After he'd gotten his clothing requirements ironed out, he left the suite and found an elevator. To his surprise, it was manned by a live operator. This was really taking ostentation to the ultimate. On the face of it, the Europeans didn't carry automation to the point they did in America. Admittedly, the operator was beyond military age, but still, if he was willing to work, why wasn't he in some defense job he could handle? Well, it was no skin off Don Mathers' nose. As soon as he could swing it, on a permanent basis, he wasn't going to be working either—ever again. He'd done his share, hadn't he? He was on record as having destroyed a Kraden cruiser.

He still didn't know how he had gotten to Paris, but evidently the fact wasn't known to either the news people or the man in the street. He passed through the lobby unrecognized. It would seem that the staff of the *Nouveau Ritz* was discreet; they knew who he was, but they weren't talking.

He told the doorman to summon a cab and within moments a hovercab was there. It wasn't automated but boasted a cabby. When Don climbed in and the driver looked back over his shoulder and his eyes widened.

Don said, "Do you understand English?"

"Oui, mon Colonel. What is your destination, mon Colonel?"

So. He was recognized. Not that it was particularly important with a hovercab driver.

Don said, "I have heard that Paris boasts the most fabulous bordellos in the world. What is the most, uh, extravagant of them all?"

The driver gaped at him. "Bordello! Pour Monsieur? But mon Colonel, you need but go to the most exclusive nightclub or bar in Paris and——"

"I know, I know," Don said impatiently. "But I have always heard of the bordellos of this city and would like to witness one. What is the most famous?"

The cabby's shrug was pure Gallic. He said, "Undoubtedly, *Le Chat Noir*, the Black Cat, Monsieur le Colonel."

"Then that's it."

They took off in wild Parisian fashion, and shortly crossed the Seine to the Left Bank after passing through the Place de la Concorde with its famed obelisk. The driver was obviously glum about their destination.

They turned left on the Boulevard Saint-Germain, turned right again on a side street and came to a halt before a rather large private house, the doorway of which was only dimly lit.

"*Le Chat Noir,*" the driver said, still disapprovingly.

Don reached for his Universal Credit Card and said, "Where's the payment slot? I've never been in a French cab before."

The other said with dignity, "Not in my taxi, mon Colonel. A holder of the Galactic Medal of Honor does not pay in my taxi. I lost a son, mon Colonel, when the *Honneur de France* blew when in orbit about Saturn two years ago."

"Oh," Don said. "Sorry. I remember hearing about it at the time." He hadn't, actually, but what could you say? He said, "Thanks, citizen."

"C'est rien," the cabby said. "It is nothing. But mon Colonel, are you sure you are safe here, all alone?"

Don said, his voice slurring slightly as a result of his accumulated drinking and the several he'd had in his suite, "My friend, I am beginning to suspect I am safe anywhere."

The driver looked back at him, "Do not be so sure, Monsieur le Colonel. Not even our Lord Jésus was safe everywhere. Without doubt, there will be some imbéciles who would tear you down."

Don was to remember his words later.

He got out of the cab, heard it take off behind him, looked at the door and grinned. "Here we go," he muttered to himself. "What can they do that you can't get elsewhere and for free?"

There was no identity screen on the door but it opened upon his approach.

He was greeted by the most improbably dressed woman he could offhand ever remember having seen. She wasn't unattractive, in spite of the fantastic amount of makeup, and appeared to be a chemical blonde of about forty-five. Her wasp-waisted red dress was of another century, her breasts all but bursting out of it, her rear, well bustled.

She began to greet him, then squinted and frowned. She said finally, "Bienvenu, Monsieur."

He followed her into an ornate sitting room and then realized the wherefore of her costume. The room was done in the decor of the Victorian period, well over a century ago. And it came to him that was the period of the famed houses of ill repute. You supposedly had to go back to the days of Babylon to equal them.

Recognition had evidently come to her, but she didn't indicate it in her words. She hesitated, momentarily, then said, in English, "If Monsieur will be seated, we will join you shortly."

Don shrugged inwardly and took a seat on a settee, which visually was one of the most baroque pieces of furniture he had ever witnessed. It wasn't the most comfortable upon which he had ever sat, either.

She left, for a moment, and then returned, smiling. She said, "Would Monsieur desire a drink . . . before?"

Before what? he wondered, but said, "Why not?"

"Cognac?"

. "Cognac sounds wonderful."

She had evidently ordered it already, since an aged servant in the costume of a nineteenth century flunky entered with a tray supporting two glasses and a squat bottle covered with dust. It was still corked and the servant, his face stolid, proceeded to open it with an old-fashioned corkscrew.

The glasses were the traditional snifter glasses, meant only for the appropriate brandy.

The woman took hers up and said, "Cheers. And, ah, what do you Americans say? What spins?"

Don tried to arise to the occasion. "My head," he said, lifting his own glass to answer the toast.

She was immediately distressed. "You are ill?"

He grinned at her sourly. "Not exactly. I have been celebrating."

She took a sip of her brandy and said approvingly, "And who has a better right?"

So, he was right, she did recognize him. He tried his. In actuality, Don Mathers had never been in a whorehouse before. They were an unknown in Center City; much too much amateur competition. The brandy was excellent. Not as good as what he had in the penthouse gardens of Lawrence Demming, of course, but unbelievably good. Guzzle wasn't particularly palatable these days, you drank for the effect, not the taste.

He said, "This is very good guzzle."

She ignored the term he used and said, "It was left to me by my grandfather. There was a note attached. He said it was to await a notable occasion. My grandfather carried the Legion of Honor, the Croix de Guerre—and various other decorations."

Don, despite being slightly drenched, tried to rise to the occasion, though in a whorehouse. He raised his glass and said, "To your grandfather and to his decorations which I am convinced he deserved manyfold."

She smiled in gratitude, lifted her own glass in answer to the toast, but said, "They were as nothing, compared to your own decoration, Monsieur."

She recognized him, all right. Evidently, in a Parisian bordello they pretended, even if they knew who you were, that they didn't. At least, they didn't use your name.

Girls began to drift into the large sitting room. And, on the face of it, they had been alerted to his identity since they were inclined to be a bit wide-eyed. They carried on the theme of the house in their dress. Some were fully clothed in much the same style as the madam. Some were in the negligee of an earlier age, some in ludicrous underwear complete to baggy bloomers, or whatever they called them.

They came in all sizes and flavors, and, by the time all had gathered, some score of them, they represented just about every type of the feminine beauty Earth produced, ranging from Sengalese ebony to the blondness of the Finns, in complexion; from overly thin to overly plump in figure; from several types of Orientals to a Black Irish girl who was possibly the most striking of all to Don's North American taste.

They took seats around the room, or draped themselves here and there in what he assumed were meant to be seductive poses. The last to enter had him gawking at first. It was a little girl, say of eleven or twelve, and she was dressed like Alice In Wonderland of the early illustrations. It wasn't until he saw her closer up that he realized that in spite of her stature and dress she was somewhat older than projected.

Twenty of them! he thought. Surely this place couldn't boast any more.

He said to his hostess, "But haven't you any other, uh, *business* tonight?

She smiled. "We sent them all away. The establishment is yours, exclusively."

"Sent them away?" he said. "How could you do that without an uproar?"

She laughed in great amusement. "I had them in-

137

formed, through the girls, that we were expecting a raid by the flics."

"Flics?"

"The police. They departed hurriedly. And now, would Monsieur, perhaps, wish to see an exhibition?"

Don Mathers had never seen an exhibition, as she called it, though he had read about them in older books. Matters involving donkeys and so forth. The fact was, particularly in America, matters pornographic were becoming all but unknown. There had been a swing of the pendulum, since the all-out days of the 60s and 70s, which had accelerated after the coming of the Kradens. The booming Universal Reformed Church had taken a particularly dim view of all-out sexual freedom. The only thing that truly mattered was the defense against the extraterrestrials and frivolity was frowned upon. Don Mathers had been raised in this atmosphere and though he had never really thought it out, subconsciously revolted against other than the standard sex practices.

"I . . . I guess not," he said, bolting back the remainder of his brandy.

She gave him another generous tot and said, "Perhaps Monsieur would rather just select two or three of the girls and . . . retire. Or perhaps Monsieur enjoys even more . . . at a time."

"Two or three?" Don said blankly, taking down another healthy gulp of fine brandy which should have been treated with more appreciation. "What would I do with two or three at a time?"

One of the platinum blondes who boasted a fabulous derriere, among other attributes, shrilled a laugh and said, with a British accent, "We know tricks."

Don cleared his throat.

The madam had a sudden inspiration and came to her feet. "Or, I know something that might intrigue Monsieur. I believe it is the only one in existence."

Don Mathers had become somewhat overwhelmed by all of this available pulchritude. He was glad to follow her.

She led him up a flight of stairs, down a corridor which continued to maintain the Victorian decor, and to a very dimly lit bedroom.

On the bed, beneath the antique canopy, was stretched a stunningly beautiful brunette, quite nude.

Madam said, "The idea was given us by a fellow American of yours. It is based on a limerick, evidently famed in your land. It begins, *There was a young man from Racine——*"

Don said hurriedly, "I've heard it." He had carried his glass with him. He took another jolt, even as he stared. "You mean, well, that's not a real girl?" he said.

She laughed, pleased with herself and the ingenuity of it all. "No, it is quite artificial, foam rubber and electric motors and so forth. However, it will perform ordinary, oral, or even anal sex. You would be surprised how popular it is with our clientele. They are invariably intrigued. Some will have none other."

Don had a sour taste in his mouth. He said, "As I recall one version of the last line of the limerick was, *But it was a hell of a thing to clean.*"

"Oh, not at all," she assured him hastily. "No difficulty whatsoever."

But that had been the first night of his stay in Paris. As in Geneva earlier, one day, one night, faded into another, and finally, together with his drinking friends, who had accumulated one by one, he was on his way back to North America. It was a well-lubricated flight.

The aircraft, one of the various devoted to high echelon brass, was lavishly equipped. It even had bedrooms and baths, though none of the party took time out to either bathe or sleep. The flight wasn't as long as all that.

Although all outranked him, and most of them considerably, Don was the focus of the party. Most of them were chairborne officers, only one or two had ever seen space duty. None had ever seen a single Kraden. Everything he said had them round-eyed.

A fleet admiral said, "Colonel Mathers, I've never

heard a detailed account of your action. Could you give us a blow by blow description?"

Don took a pull at his drink—he seldom, these days, seemed to be without a drink in his hand—and said, modestly, "Well, it all happened so fast that parts of it are blank to me."

A commodore pressed him. "The last thing we saw from the video-tapes, you had just told your admiral that you were going in, and we could see you cocking your flakflak gun. You blanked out the screen and the scanners and the next thing we saw were the shots Commodore Franco of Monitor Task Force Three took of both the Kraden wreck and your One Man Scout. Couldn't you fill us in?"

"Well . . ." Don began.

They all learned forward. One stretched forth a bottle and refilled his glass.

He said, "I came in as fast as I could and got as close as I could, figuring, I suppose, that the closer I was the more difficult it would be for them to bring their weapons to bear on me. Sometimes, I was within a meter or two of their hull."

"Almighty Ultimate," one of them muttered.

"On my first pass, I raked them from stern to bow. Then I flipped over—I have a suspicion it was the quickest turn in the history of the One Man Scout—and started back, raking them again."

"Were they firing at you?" A fleet admiral broke in.

The others scowled at him for interrupting.

But Don looked at him and frowned, as though trying to remember details. "In actuality, I don't know. I suppose so. Things were going so fast, I can't truly remember. I came back and raked them again from bow to stern. I hadn't the time to make out what effect my flakflak gun was having, if any. I wasn't sure but that their defenses were proof against anything as puny as a short beam flakflak. At any rate, I rolled and hit them again amidships, and followed completely around the whole diameter, and over and over again. I . . . well, I wasn't even aware of the fact that I'd run out of energy for the gun when Commodore Franco came up with his Monitors."

A fleet admiral laughed huskily. "You mean you were still circling him, still firing, or trying to, with an empty gun?"

Don laughed too, as though embarrassed. "Yes, sir, I guess so. I suppose I wasn't coordinating very well by that time."

"Damnedest action in military history," the commodore blurted. "It's as though a liberty launch, armed with a machine gun, had attacked and sunk the *Forrestal*."

Don looked at him questioningly.

"Before your time," the commodore said. "The *Forrestal* was the largest aircraft carrier of its day back when we had surface navies."

They landed at the Octagon airport in Bost-Wash,

said their goodbyes in great fellowship, and went their various ways.

Don Mathers considered only passingly going into Bost-Wash proper and continuing his celebration but then decided the hell with it. The prolonged binge was beginning to catch up with him. Instead, he took a commercial carrier to Center City, getting the usual attention. The stewardesses hovered over him, both the captain and co-pilot came back to shake hands, and at least a good round dozen of his fellow passengers got his autograph. He was getting used to it. He put down only a few drinks on the short trip, trying to taper off. Besides, the liquor was the standard guzzle of the day and he was already used to better things.

At the airport in Center City, he escaped the mob that gathered, got into an automated hovercab and dialed the hi-rise apartment house that contained his digs.

Once in his own mini-apartment, he looked about in contemptuous amusement. He had been gone about two weeks, but somehow it was as though it had been years. It seemed impossible that the place was *this* small and this sterile. He had always hated it. The thing was that before there had been no alternative, no point in a negative attitude.

He put down the small bag he had brought with him from Paris. He hadn't bothered to pack any of the endless clothing they had supplied him with, nor any of the guzzle, save one imperial quart of the

Scotch the President of the Solar System League had sent over.

It was hardly evening but he had the prolonged dissipation accumulated in him and touched the button that brought the bed from the wall, then ripped the civilian clothes he was wearing off and tossed them to a chair. He didn't awaken until morning.

He took his time showering and shaving, then went back into his living room, returned the bed to the wall and went over to his order box. He dialed himself a space colonel's dress uniform and for once was able to utilize his Universal Credit Card. Offhand, he couldn't remember having used it since he'd received his medal. Not even in that cathouse in Paris. Almighty Ultimate, that had been an experience. That platinum blonde hadn't been kidding when she said they knew tricks.

Dressed, he looked about the apartment and grunted contempt. It was the last night that he'd ever spend in this miniature dump.

He left the apartment and went down to the service elevators and took one to the motor pool in the basements. He wanted to avoid meeting any other residents in the building. He was beginning to get autograph signer's cramp in his right hand.

He summoned an autocab and was able to get into it quickly enough to avoid more than two handshakes and one autograph. He dialed the Interplanetary Lines Building.

By the time he had covered the distance between the curb and the huge building's entry, a small crowd had gathered and were applauding him. He grinned and waved at them, but darted inside before anyone could come up with paper and stylo.

The lobby was packed with bustling citizens to the point where nobody recognized him, which was all right with Don Mathers. He made his way over to the series of reception desks. Most of them were automated, but two boasted live girls.

The one he stopped before knew him immediately and she ogled him in surprise.

She was a cute little thing, very trim in her Interplanetary Lines uniform, which, stiff and proper though it was, failed to disguise her ripeness. She was very brunette, her black hair and brows reminding him of Dian Keramikou, her red mouth that of the German girl in Geneva, the one who was willing to put out on her honeymoon. What was her name? He couldn't remember.

He said, "I'd like to see either or both Lawrence Demming or Maximilian Rostoff."

She stood immediately. "I'll personally escort you, Colonel Mathers."

They headed for an elevator set off to one side of the public elevator banks and obviously private.

When they entered it, he grinned at her and said, "What are you doing tonight, Miss?"

Her face went pale. "Oh, anything, sir."

He grinned again. "Maybe I'll take you up on that if I'm not too busy."

He had never seen anyone so taken aback. She said, all flustered, "I'm Toni . . . Toni Fitzgerald. You can just call this building and ask for me. Any time. Any time at all."

"When are you off?"

"That doesn't make any difference, Colonel Mathers."

"Don," he said. "I wouldn't want to get you fired."

"I . . . I mean, my supervisor wouldn't dream of firing me, or anything else, if I was with you . . . Don."

"Well, maybe we'll get together," he smiled. "But meanwhile, let's see Old Man Demming."

That took her back too. She said weakly, "Mr. Demming has been out in SanSan. I don't know if he has returned as yet. But Mr. Rostoff is in his office."

SanSan, the West Coast equivalent of Bost-Wash. The city currently extended from what was once San Francisco to what was once San Diego and was still expanding, north, south and east. Only the Pacific prevented it from edging west as well.

The elevator whooshed them to rarefied altitudes and they left it to emerge into a labyrinth of extensive offices, most overrunning with computers and chattering business machines, none of which Don recognized.

"This way, Colonel Mathers," she said. "Mr. Rostoff has recently established offices in the Interplanetary Lines Building. Three floors."

He followed her, hard put to keep his eyes from her trim buttocks which managed to sway ever so slightly, despite the stiff uniform.

She said, "I've applied six times for Space Service, but they won't take me. My two brothers were lost in that collision between the *Minerva* and *Sioux City* off Pluto last year."

Don, who was to her right and very slightly behind her said, "That's too bad, Toni. However, the Space Service isn't as romantic as you might think. And the name's Don."

"Yes, sir," Toni Fitzgerald said, her soul in her eyes. "You ought to know . . . Don. Nobody will ever believe me when I tell them you told me to call you by your first name."

Don Mathers was somehow irritated, though he didn't know why. He said nothing further until they had reached their destination in the gigantic office building. He thanked her after she had turned him over to another receptionist.

However, his spirits had been restored by the time he was brought to the door of Max Rostoff's private office. His new guide, as impressed as had been Toni, hadn't even bothered to check on the interplanetary magnate's availability before ushering Mathers into the other's presence.

Max Rostoff looked up from his half acre of desk, looking wolfishly aggressive as ever.

He came to his feet, smiling, and extended a hand to be shaken. "Why, Colonel," he said, turning on such charm as he could muster. "How fine to see you again. Nora, that will be all."

Nora gave the interplanetary hero one more long worshipful look and then turned and left.

As soon as the door had closed behind her, Max Rostoff turned on his visitor and snarled, "Where have you been, you rummy sonofabitch?"

X

He couldn't have shocked Don Mathers more if he had suddenly levitated and flown out a window.

"We've been looking for you for over a week," Rostoff snapped, enraged. "Out of one bar, into another. Our men couldn't catch up with you. Dammit, don't you realize we've got to get going, you drunk? We've got a double dozen and more of documents for you to sign. We've got to get this thing underway, before somebody else does."

Don blurted, "You can't talk to me that way!"

It was the other's turn to stare. Obviously, Max Rostoff had as short a temper as his power was long. He said, low and dangerously, "No? Why can't I?"

Don glared at him.

Max Rostoff ran a hard hand back over his bald, tanned head and sneered, low and dangerously, "Let's get this straight, Mathers. To everybody else but Demming and me, you might be the biggest hero in the solar system. But you know what the hell you are to us?"

Don felt his indignation seeping from him. For the past two weeks he had been a god. For the past few days, he had begun to believe it himself. But here he was confronting reality.

Rostoff was saying, "To us, you're just another demi-buttocked incompetent on the make. You're a guzzler. A woman chaser. An opportunist willing to freeload on all the starry-eyed slobs who think you're the greatest thing to come down the aisle since Alexander the Great. You think our men didn't check you out? Hell, you didn't even pay your hovercabs. Underpaid cabbies who needed the couple of pseudo-dollars you owed them. Hell, you didn't even pay in the whorehouse you spent twenty-four hours in, in Paris. The madam closed the place up to all customers as long as you were there. Do you know who her husband was? I won't bother to tell you. He died in a One Man Scout; blew when the shuttle was taking him into orbit."

Don sank into one of the enormous office's huge, real-leather chairs.

Rostoff said, "You're a rummy and a con man and . . . a coward. We have the record of your past six patrols, Mathers."

Don said nothing. He was breathing deeply.

Rostoff added contemptuously, "Make no mistake, Mathers, you'll continue to have a good thing out of this only so long as we can use you."

A voice from behind them said, "Let me add to that, period, end of paragraph." It was the corpulent Lawrence Demming, who had just waddled in from an inner office.

He said, and even his voice seemed fat, "And now that's settled, I'm going to call in some of our lawyers who have already begun to work on the project. While they are about, we conduct ourselves as though we're three equals. Theoretically we will be." He lowered himself into a sizable chair with a sigh. It was obvious that his feet were too small for his bulk.

"Wait a minute now," Don blurted. "What do you mean theoretically? What in the hell do you think you're pulling? The agreement was we split this whole thing three ways."

Demming's jowls wobbled as he nodded. "That's right. And your share of the loot is your Galactic Medal of Honor. That and the dubious privilege of having the whole thing in your name. You'll keep your medal and we'll keep our share." He grunted heavily and added, "You don't think you're getting the short end of the stick, do you?"

"I think I'm getting shafted with the stick," Don said indignantly.

Rostoff had reseated himself. He said now, "Let's keep this on as gentlemanly a scale as possible." He took Don in. "We've been working this over ever since you were successful in your farce attack upon the Kraden. This is what we've come up with. We are going immediately to incorporate the Donal Mathers Radioactives Mining Corporation, concentrating at first on Callisto and its pitchblende deposits. Recent prospecting has indicated a high incidence of carnotite on Ganymede and Io. We'll undoubtedly move in on them."

"What's carnotite?" Don said, his voice sulky.

Rostoff's face indicated disgust at the other's lack of knowledge. "It's an ore composed of oxides of vanadium, uranium and potassium. It usually occurs, often in cavities of rocks, as a lemon-yellow crystalline powder; it crystallizes in the orthorhombic system."

Don Mathers was out of his depth. "All right, go on," he said. "What's all this about my being squeezed out?"

"That's not the way to put it," Demming wheezed. He had closed his eyes and leaned back into his chair as Rostoff talked.

Rostoff went on. "We're going to present this on the highest patriotic level," he said. "The Donal Mathers Radioactives Mining Corporation is above such mundane matters as making large profits. You will be president and you'll be chairman of the board, but you will not own a single share of stock. That should impress the peasants."

"What the hell do I live on?" Don said with belligerence.

"All that you will receive from the corporation will be your expenses. Of course, your expense account will be unlimited. You will receive not a single pseudo-dollar in salary, but what difference if your expense account is unlimited?"

"The same thing," Demming wheezed.

"What's the Space Service going to say about all this?" Don said. "Officers aren't supposed——"

"You'll resign from the Space Service tomorrow," Rostoff said.

"That won't go over. You're not allowed to resign, especially in time of war. Besides, it'll hurt my image with the common herd."

Rostoff made with a humorless laugh. "No, it won't. In the first place, you can resign any time you want. You can do no wrong. In the second place, we've assembled a whole squad of writers and speech writers for you. This will be presented as the ultimate in patriotism, you throwing yourself into a non-profit endeavor to solve the uranium shortage."

Demming said, "You'd better move into my apartments. Tomorrow the speech writers want a preliminary session with you. They want your style of talking. They're going to have to work on your public image. We also have a couple of actors to coach you. Then you'll have to have a session with the makeup staff."

"Makeup!"

"Yes," Rostoff said. "Everything from the way you cut your hair to the type of civilian clothes you wear. We're considering a new style of clothes, which you'll sponsor. The simplicity look. You're going to be the clean-cut kid from next door, who, in view of the war effort, scorns expensive, fancy clothing, expensive cars, and all the rest of it."

"Almighty Ultimate, why?"

Rostoff sighed. "The standard of living is too damn high these days. To maintain it, employees have to be paid too much. We want to lower wages and salaries—all in the name of the war effort, of course. We're going to get them down to a living wage."

"A meager living wage," Demming said. "The bastards are living too high on the hog."

Look who's talking about hogs, Don thought inwardly.

Rostoff said, "In the privacy of your own quarters, of course, you can do whatever you want. Eat, drink, wear, and bed anything or anybody you want. But in public you're a simple, earnest, personally unambitious young man, as befits being the hero of the solar system."

Demming sighed satisfaction and said, "The common stock we sell will return a minimum dividend, very minimum. The dividends of the preferred stock will be limited only by the rate of profit the corporation realizes. Max, here, and I will own the preferred stock but that fact will not be made public. Through you, we will take measures to get permission to withhold such information due to, ah, let us say, national security, always a useful term."

"It's the rip-off of the century," Don muttered.

Rostoff grinned his wolf grin. "It's the rip-off of all history," he corrected.

"And you called me a con man," Don said bitterly.

Demming wheezed again and said, "Let's knock this off and get the law boys in." He pushed his bulk to his feet and went over to the desk and flicked a switch on one of the screens there and said, "Dirck."

Dirck Bosch, his Belgian secretary, entered from the same inner office Demming had emerged from earlier.

Demming said, "Bring in the damn lawyers. We've got enough paper work to keep us busy for the rest of the week."

Don said, "Wait a minute. What if I say no?"

Rostoff chuckled his humorless laugh. He said, "We four here, including you, are the only living persons who know that you're a heel, not a hero."

Don Mathers lost track of the number of lawyers who came and went. They were all obviously top men in their various fields, very deferential to Demming and Rostoff and as impressed with meeting Don as anybody else had been since his decoration. Two of them, pleading children who collected, even asked for autographs. Don, of course, complied, suspecting that they, in actuality, wanted them for themselves, not for their kids.

It would be impossible for him to ever go broke,

he decided acidly. If worse came to worse, he could always stand on a street corner and sell his signature for, say five pseudo-dollars a throw.

He didn't bother to read any of the things he signed. Had he, it would have taken him forever, some of the sheafs of legal paper were half an inch thick.

Finally, Demming grunted to his secretary, "What time is it, Dirck?"

Dirck Bosch told him immediately, seemingly not even looking at his wrist chronometer.

Demming lurched to his feet. "I have a guest," he said. "Let's call the rest of this off until tomorrow."

Rostoff said, "Tomorrow, Don is going to have to start work on his autobiography."

"Autobiography?" Don snorted. "I could no more write an autobiography than——"

Rostoff said absently, scanning some papers in his hands, "We've got a writer chap to ghost it. One of the best authors in the system. But he'll have a lot of questions to ask you. We want to get it into print as soon as possible—before we issue stock. We're also having two other books done, one a juvenile, another a straight biography."

Demming was headed for an elevator to one side of the room. He said, "I'll go up and welcome the Grand Presbyter. Max, can you stay for dinner?"

"Yes, of course."

Demming said to Don, "We have a suite prepared

for you. You can pick up your things, or we'll have one of the men go over to get them, tomorrow. I'll expect you gentlemen in ten minutes or so. In the blue dining room, Max."

Maximilian Rostoff and Don wound up two or three more items and then the lawyers left, followed by the self-effacing Dirck Bosch, leaving Rostoff and Don alone.

Don looked at the door through which the Belgian secretary had just gone and said, "What spins with him?"

Rostoff didn't look up but said, "Who?"

"Bosch. He knows the whole story. Suppose he spills it?"

Rostoff shook his head. "Demming owns him. Some years ago he worked in Demming's, let us say, security staff. A situation arose in which it became necessary to, as you'd say, liquidate two financial competitors. Demming has definite proof that Bosch performed the deed." He smiled his lupine smile. "The moral of the story is, don't ever let friend Lawrence get anything on you. Which, obviously, is too late a warning in your case."

Don said, "He could still spill, given enough pressure of whatever sort on him. He hates Demming."

"Everybody hates Demming. You're more observant than I would have given you credit for. However, Bosch has a semi-invalid wife and two children in Brussels. Their only source of income is

Bosch's pay from Demming. Her medical bills are high. If anything happened to Bosch's income they would be in poverty."

"He could get a job somewhere else, if he could beat the murder rap. He's obviously a top notch man."

"Not with Demming blacklisting him. Let's go on upstairs. You're going to meet the Grand Presbyter."

"The Grand Presbyter! You mean the head of the Universal Reformed Church? I thought I misunderstood Demming when he mentioned this guest of his."

Rostoff didn't bother to answer. He tossed the legal papers to his desk and led the way to the elevator.

When the door opened again, they emerged into a dining room possibly half again as large as the "cozy" family room in which he had eaten with the Demming family several weeks before. It was largely in blue, even the Gainsborough painting which Don absently recognized as that master's most famous work. He wondered how many dining rooms Demming maintained in all.

Besides Martha and Alicia Demming, there was a stranger present. Not exactly a stranger. Don recognized him from the times he had seen him on Tri-Di. It was Peter Fodor, Grand Presbyter of the Universal Reformed Church, successor to the prominence once held by a combination of the Pope, the

Patriarch of the Orthodox Eastern Church, and the
Grand Mufti of Mecca. He was a quiet, dignified
man in his early sixties. He was very straight in pos-
ture and slight in build though his comparatively
simple robes did little to hide a rounded paunch.
He held a glass of sherry in his hand, as did Martha
and Alicia. Somewhat to Don's surprise, there was a
quirk of sly humor in his eyes that didn't show up
on Tri-Di where he usually seemed somewhat sad.

Upon Don and Rostoff's appearance, Lawrence Demming bustled over, beaming. He took
Don by the arm in friendly fashion and led him to
where Peter Fodor and the ladies were chatting.

"Your Supreme Holiness," he said, "may I present
our solar system hero, Colonel Donal Mathers?"

The Grand Presbyter put out a hard dry hand.

Don didn't know if he was supposed to kiss it or
shake it. He wasn't a member of the Universal Reformed Church, nor any other, for that matter—if
there were any others left. He wasn't up on matters religious. He shook.

Peter Fodor said, "My son, surely the Almighty
Ultimate was at your side when you attacked the
Kraden monsters." His voice was strong but still
held a kindly ring.

"I . . . I suppose so, Your Supreme Holiness," Don
got out.

"A touch of Amontillado, Colonel Mathers?"
Demming wheezed, still beaming fondly at Don.

"Why, yes sir," Don said. "Thank you." He hadn't

had a drink all day and could use one in view of the developments of the past hours.

His host must have made some imperceptible signal since a liveried servant came hurrying up with a gold tray upon which was a superlatively beautiful crystal decanter and a sherry glass. Demming himself took up the container and poured. He handed the glass to Don.

Rostoff had ordered his own drink from one of the servants. By the looks of it, it was a double shot of very cold vodka. He slugged it back in one bolt, put the glass down and came over to join the others.

The two women were gushing over Don—if it could be said that the bland Martha was capable of gushing. However, she did her best in her rasping voice.

Now, once again, Alicia Demming was another thing. She was wearing a golden formal dress, with no jewelry save a magnificent emerald necklace, and it set off her fine blond hair and green eyes to perfection.

She was saying, "Good heavens, Colonel Mathers, father must be clairvoyant, or whatever they call it when you can look into the future. Imagine! The last time we saw you, you were a mere sub-lieutenant. Now you are the toast of the Solar System."

"Sheer luck, Ms. Demming," Don said with befitting modesty.

"I am sure not," His Supreme Holiness said. "Your courage and gallantry are an example for all our noble young warriors fighting for the Almighty Ultimate and his highest creation, the human race."

"Most certainly," Maximilian Rostoff said, with great conviction.

Alicia had that starry look in her eye that Don was getting used to in young women, and not-so-young women, for that matter.

She said to him, "Alicia, not Ms. Demming . . . Don."

At table, Don remembered the last siege he'd had in this home and took it easy on each course and with each wine. He didn't want to become foundered again.

Demming was saying to him, "It is a great privilege to have his Supreme Holiness here. He has decided to throw the full weight of the Universal Reformed Church into our efforts to amalgamate system-wide efforts to produce radioactives for the war effort. The church will proclaim the need for sacrifice from every citizen."

"We will proclaim a *jihad*," the Grand Presbyter said, his voice inspired.

Don regarded him blankly. "A what?"

"A *jihad*," the other told him definitely. "It comes down from the Arabic, when the scimitar was conquering half the civilized world under the inspiration of the Prophet. The Moslem world, of course, is now all but completely assimilated into the Universal Reformed Church, but it is fitting that we proclaim a Holy War against the Kraden monsters."

Rostoff said, his voice only very faintly wry, "To help subsidize it, we are issuing His Supreme Holiness two percent of the preferred stock of the Donal Mathers Radioactives Mining Corporation."

Alicia said, taking her eyes from Don momentarily, "You mean you're actually going to donate two percent of the corporation stock to the Universal Reformed Church, father?" On the face of it, Alicia Demming had never heard of her father ever having freely donated anything to anybody.

Lawrence Demming pursed his plum lips judiciously. "Not exactly, my dear. The stock will be issued to Peter Fodor, the Grand Presbyter, in his own name. We have decided that in this manner he will be in a position to more efficiently handle the income. Indeed, we do not plan to release the information to the media."

"Much more efficient," Rostoff said.

His Supreme Holiness said benignly, "It will give me considerably more leeway. Unnecessary to go through red-tape and church hierarchy channels to accomplish immediate results."

Inwardly, Don Mathers wondered what two percent of, say, a few hundred billion was.

Martha Demming said to Don sweetly, in an obvious make-conversation gambit, "And what is your mining background, Colonel Mathers?"

Demming looked at her from the side of his eyes, and then closed them in pain momentarily, before opening them again so that he could resume plowing into the brace of capons before him.

Rostoff took over gently, explaining, "The Colonel will not deal with such mundane matters as the technology involved in extracting uranium and other radioactives, Ms. Demming. He will work on the highest levels of policy, high echelon decisions, public relations, that sort of thing."

"Oh, I see. My, such responsibility for such a young man."

She gave Don a bucktoothed, approving smile, and he inwardly winced.

After the ladies had withdrawn, the four men took to cigars and port. Don was treated, by his two supposed partners, as an equal. Indeed, if anything, they deferred to him. His opinion was always carefully listened to and the both of them would sagely nod whenever he made a point. Which was, however, seldom enough since he knew nothing whatsoever about corporation law and even less about radioactives, beyond their use in the nuclear engines of a One Man Scout.

Somewhat to his surprise, His Supreme Holiness *was* up on corporation law and fully able to discuss fine points with his host and Rostoff. Indeed, after a flurry of discussion on one phase of the development of Don's new corporation, Demming and Rostoff excused themselves, came to their feet, and, cigars in hand, went over to the terrace, which overlooked Center City, from its lofty altitude, and conferred in low voices.

The Grand Presbyter tapped ash from his imperial size Manila cigar. Don had understood that the Universal Reformed Church frowned upon, though it did not completely forbid, use by the faithful of tobacco and alcohol. Evidently, His Supreme Holiness was making an exception tonight.

He said, "Have you ever considered taking Holy Orders, my son?"

XI

Don stared at him and took a hasty slug of his port. "Doing what?"

"Taking Holy Orders. We could elevate you to a Missionary Apostle. I would think that it would aid immeasurably in bringing new converts to the Church, and, of course, the greater our membership the greater the number to participate in our *jihad* against the Kradens."

"Well, no," Don said, less than happy. "You see, I am not even a member of the Universal Reformed Church. My parents weren't religious whatsoever, so I wasn't raised in the atmosphere."

"Then, my son, you are not acquainted with the tenets of the Church?"

"Not at all. And, I'm a space pilot. Wouldn't it look rather far out if suddenly I became a, what did you call it, a Missionary Apostle?"

His Supreme Holiness shook his head, after taking another appreciative pull at his dark cigar. "Not at all, my son. Haven't you ever heard of the Loyola story?"

"I don't believe so."

"Briefly, Ignatius of Loyola was born in the 15th Century and was of noble background. As a youth he left his life at court and joined the military. He distinguished himself in many actions and was also known to be a great, hmmm, lady's man and carouser. Indeed, it is said that his broken leg, which caused him to limp the rest of his life, was a result of his having to jump from a paramour's window upon the arrival of her husband."

His Supreme Holiness chuckled, as though he was being very bold. "However, during his convalescence from either this wound or another, he was converted through reading a life of Christ. After deep studies he, with six friends, took vows of poverty and chastity and were later ordained. They formed a new order, the Society of Jesus, or Jesuits, and it became one of the most effective religious organizations the world has ever seen. After his death, he was canonized in 1622."

Don was uncomfortable. It was obvious that the Grand Presbyter was considered of great importance to the corporation by Demming and Rostoff or they wouldn't have let him into the inner circles of the deal. However, Don Mathers had no intention of taking Holy Orders. He had every intention of living it up for the rest of his life.

He said, "You mentioned that he spent years of study. I am afraid that my duties as head of the

Radioactives Mining Corporation wouldn't allow me much time for study."

"Ah, my son, the tenets of our modern Church are not so complicated as all that. Basically, our raison d' etre is that half a century ago thinking persons began to desert the organized churches of the time. Which is not strange, in view of the fact that such organizations as the Jewish, Christian, Mohammedan and Buddhist were initiated long centuries ago, indeed, millennia ago. They were conceived by nomads and, anthropologically speaking, by barbarians. Obviously, their teachings do not make a great deal of sense to a modern, educated, civilized man."

"Such as what, for example?" Don said, just to be saying something.

"Let us take an extreme case. According to the Bible, accepted by Jews, Christians and even Mohammedans, though to a lesser degree, God created man in his own image. This is obviously nonsense to a modern, educated man. Man's body is suited to his environment, the Earth. And God's? Does God have a penis? If so, why? What does he do with it? Does he have an anal passage? Does he have a navel? If so, why? Does he have teeth? If so, what does he bite with them? Does he have the sense organs, eyes, ears, nose? Why? An omniscient being would not need to utilize the sense organs necessary on the surface of Earth."

"I suppose you're right," Don said.

"Not even some of the basic tenets hold up too well. Take the story of the Ten Commandments. Supposedly, Moses went up Mt. Sinai and there confronted God. By the way, there is a bit of humor here. Moses requested to see God's face, but was informed it was much too holy for him to see. However, God allowed him to glimpse his "nether parts" as it is worded. Why the buttocks of the Supreme Being should be any less holy than His face, is difficult to understand. At any rate, the Ten Commandments were engraved upon a stone and Moses carried them down to the people. By the way, what language were they written in? The Hebrews had no written language at that time. Perhaps in hieroglyphics? The Egyptian picture writing of the time was not exactly conducive to projecting such ideas as the Ten Commandments. I suggest that you reread them, one of these days. They are not all that inspiring to a modern man. Most of them deal with the fact that you should worship Jehovah and none other. He presents himself as somewhat vain."

"For instance?" Don said. As a matter of fact, when he had been a student when matters religious would come up, he would often say, "I'm an agnostic but I believe in the Ten Commandments."

"For instance, *Honor thy father and thy mother*," the other said somewhat cynically. "But suppose that they are not deserving of honor? Suppose one is a habitual drunkard who beats you and the other a syphilitic prostitute who brought you into the world blind as a result of her disease?"

The Grand Presbyter went on. "Or, *Thou shall not kill.* Including Kradens? Down through history man has killed, including, and possibly especially, in religious wars.

"And just how up-to-date are such commandments as, *Thou shalt not covet thy neighbor's ass?*" There was a very slight leer on the religious leader's face. "Unless, of course, the commandment was referring to homosexuality."

Don stared at him. He got out, "Pardon me, Your Supreme Holiness, but I'll be darned if you sound very devout."

The other put down his cigar and took up his glass of port. He said wryly, "My son, it has been said that the more one knows of one's religion, the less one believes. However, I have not been speaking of my religion but of the old and antiquated ones. Our religion fits modern conditions. We do not envision an improbably man-like God who comes down to Earth and strolls about punishing those who do not worship him wholeheartedly, unthinkingly. We believe in evolution, not creation, though possibly we acceed to the fact that the Almighty Ultimate directed evolution. We are strong on the acceptable teachings of the old religions, such as the Golden Rule, but we scorn the anachronistic."

Demming and Rostoff were returning from the terrace.

The Grand Presbyter said, "Think about it. I am of the belief that your taking Holy Orders would do our common, hmmm, interest much good."

"Okay," Don said.

Demming said, "The ladies will be in the Gold Room. Shall we join them, Your Supreme Holiness, Colonel Mathers, Max?"

The Gold Room adjoined the Blue Dining Room and, of course, the motif was golden, even including the frames which housed the Renaissance paintings on the walls. Once again, Don Mathers was no connoisseur of either furniture or art objects, but it came off to him as on the gaudy side.

The ladies were seated and had small liqueur glasses before them. In keeping with the room, Alicia's drink seemed to contain specks of gold suspended in a water-colored liquid that could have been gin or vodka. Don couldn't help stare at it, as the three men came up.

The girl laughed. "It's *Goldwasser*, Colonel Mathers . . . ah, Don. A cordial that comes from Danzig. It's fascinating to look at but, in truth, a bit too sweet. They are real tiny flakes of gold. One must shake up the bottle just before serving, since the gold slowly settles to the bottom."

"I learn something every day," Don said.

All laughed, or at least smiled.

The conversation became lighter than it had been when the four men were by themselves, but shortly the Grand Presbyter checked his wrist chronometer and looked up, as though in regret.

"I am afraid my morning duties are such that I must leave," he said. "It has been a most enjoyable evening." His eyes went to Demming and Rostoff. "And I trust a most profitable one as a result of our decisions."

Demming lumbered to his feet, summoned a servant from one of the several who hovered in the background, and, after His Supreme Holiness had made his goodbyes to the others, led him to the room's elevator. Seemingly, there was an elevator door in every room in the house, Don decided. It was the damnedest system he had ever come up against.

After the Grand Presbyter and his servant guide had gone, Don said, "You know, I should get to bed myself. From what you say, I've got a busy day tomorrow, and, first of all, I'm going to have to report at the spaceport. I imagine Command is going to be wondering where in the world I am, although they've made no attempt to contact me."

Demming huffed, "Have you any preference as to your accommodations here, Donal? The type of suite in which you would feel most at home?"

It hadn't occurred to Don that he would have a selection. He had expected simply to be assigned a room.

He said, "Why, actually, if it makes no difference

to you, I'd like to stay up in the penthouse. Your gardens are beautiful and we space pilots see little enough of trees, grass and flowers."

Alicia stood. "I'll show Don to the visitor's suite in the right wing, Father."

The others, save Martha, stood as well and Don said his goodnights. The two men were as friendly as though he was a bosom companion of long years' standing.

He followed the girl to the elevator, the door to which opened automatically at their approach. He was surprised to find the compartment available.

"Back so soon?" he said.

She laughed. "This isn't the same one the Grand Presbyter took," she explained, entering before him. He followed her and she said into the order screen, "The visitor's suite in the right wing of the penthouse."

The elevator, if elevator it could properly be called, moved sidewards for a time.

Don said, "You know, I've never even heard of an elevator of this type."

She smiled at him, seemingly glad to have him to herself for the first time this evening. She said, "It was constructed especially to father's specifications. You see, this establishment consists of the top two floors of the building and the penthouse. There are also two floors of offices below devoted entirely to father's projects. Father hates to walk. Besides, just getting about would be terribly time-consuming, if one had to. The library, for instance, must be the better part of half a kilometer from father's bedroom."

"Ultimate Almighty," Don muttered.

The compartment started upward.

He said, "You mean this shaft that we're in tunnels around to every room in the place?"

"Practically. It's very handy."

"Don't you have ordinary halls and ordinary doors?"

"Why, yes. And if only a short distance is involved we utilize them."

He said, "Does your father have this sort of layout in all of his, uh, establishments?"

"So far as I know. Possibly not in some of the smaller ones he maintains."

Don said, "Look, how many, uh, establishments does your father have, that is, that he lives in?"

She looked mystified. "Why, I haven't the slightest idea. He maintains some sort of living quarters in every really major city and also the major settlements on the satellites and Mars. Sometimes, in places he visits seldom or only briefly, it will consist of no more than an apartment sufficient for himself and his immediate staff, and possibly a few guests. You know, twenty-five rooms or so."

"Really roughs it, eh?"

The compartment had stopped and the door opened into a living room. It was done in American Colonial antiques, and done very well, looking comfortable and certainly a damn sight more acceptable than either the dining room or the Gold Room in which they had spent the evening.

As they entered, she looked up from the side of her eyes and said, "Father has a good many interests, you must realize. It is quite impractical for him to go to hotels—that sort of thing. He must have one of his staffs, his business equipment, that sort of thing, immediately available. He must also be assured of security against the efforts of his business competitors. You know, bugging."

"I suppose so," Don said, taking in the room. He had seen a good deal of luxury recently but it occurred to him that when and if he made a permanent or semi-permanent establishment of his own in the near future, he might well have it done like this.

"Like it?" she said. "If it doesn't appeal to you, there are other suites."

"I like it very much."

"Thank you. I designed it, selected the furniture, the paintings and so forth. Do you like Grant Wood?"

He hadn't the slightest idea of who Grant Wood was. He said, "You're an interior decorator?"

"An amateur. I have to find something to fill my time."

He looked about. "Isn't there an autobar? We could have a nightcap."

Alicia shook her head. "No there isn't. I don't like

autobars. I don't much like automated things in general."

She went over to what he had taken to be a bookcase and pressed something. The false front slid to one side. Behind was a large selection of bottles, glasses, bar equipment and even a small refrigeration compartment.

She said, over her shoulder, "What would you like?"

He said, "Holy smokes, where does your father get all this fancy guzzle of his?"

She sighed and said, "When it comes to food and drink, father doesn't exactly stint himself. He has agents who continually comb the world seeking out the best potables still remaining. He'll pay anything."

"You mean he's got collections like this in all of his, uh, establishments?"

"Yes, but this is nothing. This is just for temporary visitors, guests. Down below, he has extensive cellars. There is more guzzle in this building alone than he, and all his guests, could drink in a lifetime. Father hoards the things that mean the most to him, exotic foods, drink . . . and money."

Don said, "Surprise me."

She took down a long bottle. "This is a stone-age Metaxa." It was sealed. She took up a small bar knife, cut away the lead shielding of the cork, then took up a corkscrew. Alicia Demming had opened bottles before.

Don had never seen a real cork before he had met Demming. They were a thing of the past.

"What's Metaxa?" he said.

"Greek brandy. When it's very old, it's as good a brandy as there is. Quite different from French cognac, though."

She half filled two snifter glasses for them. It was a rugged charge.

They took the drinks back to a couch and seated themselves comfortably, about two feet from each other.

Don sipped at the brandy. He had sampled some of the best guzzle in the world in the past couple of weeks. It hadn't made him blasé.

He said easily, "You don't particularly like your father, do you?"

She said, "I don't believe I know anybody that does." And then, after a sip at her Greek brandy, "What in the world are you doing, working with him and that vicious Max Rostoff?"

So. She wasn't in on the secret. And he had to assume that her mother wasn't either. Without doubt, the two tycoons were keeping every one in the dark, so far as the real nature of Don's decoration was concerned. Which was obviously good sense. He felt that it behooved him to be careful now.

He said, "I suppose that my run-in with the Kraden cruiser made me see the light clearer than I ever had before. I've come to the conclusion that

the only chance the human race has is to unite as
never before in the face of a common foe."

"Cheers, cheers," she said, as she lifted her glass,
and he didn't know if there was an element of sarcasm there or not. "But what's all this got to do
with my father and Max Rostoff?"

He said carefully, "Probably our single biggest
need is for an abundant supply of uranium for our
space fleet. Your father and Rostoff are two of the
wealthiest men in the solar system. It will need that
kind of wealth to amalgamate all efforts to exploit
the pitchblende and other sources of uranium in the
satellites."

She yawned. "What does father get out of it? I've
never seen him go into anything that didn't net
one hundred percent a year."

Don said, still carefully, "Your father will, of
course, realize dividends. But that's the socioeconomic system we live under. Someone is going to
make a good deal of money. Why shouldn't it be
him? He's a competent businessman with a huge
staff to help him."

She said softly, "What do you get out of it, Don?"

"Nothing."

She looked at him sceptically. "How do you
mean?"

"I own no stock. I receive no salary. My efforts
are voluntary." That was telling her.

"I see," she said. "Why?"

This had to be good and, besides, he suspected

that he was going to have to tell the story over and over again in the coming months and years. He had better get it down pat.

He said, "So far as I am concerned, Alicia, I died out there. There was no reason for me to expect to continue living. There wasn't a chance in the world that I'd survive. But I did. I feel that I am living on borrowed time. And I expect to devote the rest of my life, borrowed as it is, to defeating the Kradens." Once, again, that was laying it on the line sincerely.

Without expression, she finished her drink and said, "You mentioned a busy day tomorrow, shouldn't you be getting to bed?"

He put his own glass down. "I suppose so. Where is the bedroom?"

She said, "Over here," and led the way to a door. Even as she walked, she reached up to undo the shoulder strap of her golden gown.

Don blinked but said, "If you don't like your father, why do you live here?"

"I don't. I spend almost all of my time abroad. I came back to attend my mother's fifty-fifth birthday. That's when I met you, before. Then, after your defeat of the Kraden, father dropped the information that you would be returning to see him. So I stayed on."

"Why?" he said.

"Because I wanted to go to bed with you," she told him, letting her dress drop to her waist, even as she entered the bedroom.

That set back even Don Mathers.

And for more reasons than one. Among other things, he suspected that an operator such as Lawrence Demming would have even visitors' rooms in his home bugged.

He said, virtuously, though his mouth was dry at the revealing of the upper portion of her fabulous body, "Look, I'm a guest in your father's home. What would he think of my seducing his daughter?"

She turned to face him and her expression was mocking. "But you bear the Galactic Medal of Honor."

He let air out of his lungs.

"And, besides," she said, still mockingly, "who's seducing whom?"

XII

When they awoke the next morning, she turned to him and said, "Would you consider marrying me?"

He stared over at her. "What?"

"I said, would you consider marrying me?"

"It never occurred to me. Why would someone in your position want to?"

She put her slim hands behind her head and stared up at the ceiling. "Why not? You're nice looking and possibly the most eligible young man in the Solar System. You're good in bed and . . . I like you."

"And you're one of the richest heiresses going. How come you haven't already married? Surely you must have had a lot of opportunity."

"Because I'm one of the richest heiresses in the system. Do you realize what that means? Half of the young men I meet would like to marry me for my money. The other half would like to marry me because they are already rich but would like to merge their fortune with mine and emerge possibly the most financially powerful magnate in the solar system. I never meet a man I don't suspect of one of those two alternatives."

"Why me?" Don Mathers was bewildered.

"Because you have proven that you have no interest in money. If you had you wouldn't be contributing your efforts voluntarily, without even pay, to what will possibly be the largest single corporation in the system. I will know, if you marry me, that it is because you love me and want me—no other motivation."

Don remained silent for a long moment. This was one for the book. It'd certainly be a joke on old Demming if he did marry the girl. The bastard had squeezed Don out of the stock ownership.

She misunderstood his silence and said, a shy quality there that didn't go with her usual aristocratic aloofness, "I'm not pressing you. I realize that you've got to think it over. You hardly know me and you've already mentioned that it has only been a couple of months since your engagement was broken. And you must remember that very likely she now regrets it, since you are the toast of the race."

That hadn't occurred to Don Mathers. That Dian Keramikou might now be seeing him in a new light. Now that he did think about it, he realized that very possibly, there on Callisto, Dian was having people ask for her autograph, in view of the fact that she had once been engaged to him. He almost laughed.

He swung his legs over the side of the bed to the floor and sat up. He had to play this very earnestly now, no matter what decision he made.

He said, "You're very sweet Alicia, and certainly this has been the most memorable night I have ever spent. However, as you say, we hardly know each other. I suggest that we *both* think about it."

She remained in the bed, one of the black sheets up to her neck, as he went into the bath and showered and used depilatory on his face.

She watched him, her startling green eyes thoughtful, as he went to the closet for his clothes.

When he brought the uniform forth, she said, "Oh, good heavens, Don. You don't want to wear that again. Just leave it there. One of the servants will pick up after you. There's an order box in the dressing room, over there. Order fresh clothing."

He looked at her. "I've only worn it once."

"Once is enough," she said, yawning.

"Don't you ever wear anything more than once?"

"Seldom," she said. "Only if it has some sentimental value, or something."

He shrugged and went into the dressing room, to the screen of the large order box, and verbally ordered a fresh colonel's uniform and the haberdashery to go with it.

When he had dressed, he went back to the bedroom and bent over and kissed her. If anything, she looked more beautiful than ever with her hair mussed every which way and her cosmetics a victim of the night's tussling.

"Thank you," he said simply and turned and left.

In the living room he approached the elevator door which opened automatically at his approach. Before he could say anything into the screen, it said, "There is a message for you, Colonel Mathers. A hover-limousine awaits you on the lawn."

He had planned to go down to the motor pool in the basements of the Interplanetary Lines Building and take a hovercab to the space base.

But he said, "All right. Take me there." He probably would have had his work cut out finding his way from the building. It was possibly small by the standards that applied to Lawrence Demming, but it was a labyrinth to Don Mathers.

The compartment moved sideways, for not too great a way, and then the door opened. He found himself looking out upon the extensive gardens, the groves of trees and the lawns, of the unbelievable park Demming had built atop his building.

He wasn't too far from the terrace upon which he had first met Demming and Rostoff. The hover-limousine was even parked in approximately the same spot.

Cockney was standing next to the vehicle, holding the rear door open. His partner was up front at the controls.

Frank Cockney, his bluish lips in his thin face trying to make with a smile, said, "Good morning, Colonel Mathers. We've been instructed to take you to the base."

"All right," Don said, getting in.

The other hesitated before saying, "And congratulations on your victory, Colonel. There's never been anything like that before. Ever."

"Thanks," Don said. So these two weren't in on the secret either. Which was good, of course. It would seem that they were part of Demming's security staff. Bodyguards, in other words.

Cockney got into the front, next to the other goon and the vehicle took to the air in a swoop.

On the way to the base, Frank Cockney turned and said to Don, "You know, Colonel. I never would have dreamed when we saw you that last time, you'd wind up the biggest hero in the solar system."

"Neither did I," Don said.

Cockney said, "You know, I never could figure out why Mr. Demming wanted to talk to you. He must've had some instinct, like, that big things were going to happen to you."

"He's a smart man, all right."

Cockney frowned, as though in puzzlement. "But how could he have known you'd pull the big one, and finally it'd wind up with this big corporation?"

"What big corporation?" Don said warily.

"Oh, everybody knows about that."

Don said, making it clear he didn't want to continue the conversation. "It's still unannounced.

We're supposed to keep everything quiet for the time."

Cockney said, "Yes, sir. I wasn't trying to pry." He turned back in his seat, obviously unhappy.

Don had expected to be left off at the main gate and to have to proceed to the administration buildings on a hovercart, but to his surprise the limousine flew right onto the base grounds. Evidently, Demming's vehicles had clearance.

"Where to, Colonel?" Cockney said.

"To the Space Command Headquarters, Third Division. It's over——"

"Yes, sir," the pilot said, his voice as expressionless as his heavy face. "I know where it is." Don remembered his name, Bil Golenpaul.

They slithered up before the main entry of the administration building and Golenpaul set it down, gently. If nothing else, he was a competent pilot.

Cockney popped out and ran around to open Don's door.

"Yes, sir," he said. "We'll wait, right here."

Don said, "No. Go on back. I don't know how long I'll be."

"Our orders were to wait and bring you back, when you got through with your business, Colonel Mathers."

Don looked at him. "And my orders are that you get out of here. I'm not sure that I'm going back. Not immediately."

Cockney's faded eyes shifted, in furtive fashion. He said, "But our orders. . . ."

Don was feeling belligerent. He said, "Get out of here or I'll call over that squad of guards and have you thrown out."

The small man looked at him in dismay. "Yes, sir," he said. He climbed back into the hover-limousine looking apprehensive. Don assumed he was worrying about what to tell Demming.

Well, the hell with Demming. It was bad enough having to live in his establishment, as Alicia called it. He wasn't going to put up with the other dictating every move he made.

He strode toward the entry and the squad of guards there sprang to stiff salute, presenting their laser rifles with precision. Inwardly, Don was amused. He had gone through these portals hundreds of times before and not a guard had ever batted an eye at him, not to speak of coming to attention.

Their lieutenant approached him and saluted snappily. "Could I be of assistance, Colonel?"

Don smiled and said, "No thanks, Lieutenant. I know my way around."

The other was a few years younger than Don Mathers. He said, admiration in his voice. "You certainly do, sir." He stepped aside.

The doors opened and Don entered and retraced the route he had been over so many times.

But this time was with a difference. The hustle and bustle dropped off. The chatter of the voco-typers and other electronic business machine equipment fell away. He could hear a multitude of whispers and even made out some of them.

"That's him. . . ."

"Holy Moses, the Galactic Medal of Honor. . . ."

And a feminine voice, "How would you like to be able to date *him*, Gracie . . . ?"

Doors opened magically before him. Guards presented arms, rather than asking for identification. If there was anyone in the solar system not acquainted with his face by this time, they must have been in remote areas indeed.

Eventually, he stood before his immediate commander, Commodore Walt Bernklau. Don came to attention and tossed the other a snappy salute.

The commodore returned it, just as snappily, and leaned his small body back in his swivel chair. He said, "Take a seat, Colonel. It's nice to see you you again." He added, pleasantly, "Where in the world have you been?"

Don slumped into the indicated chair and said wearily, "On a bust, sir. The bust to end all busts. Wine, women and song—and I spent precious little time on the latter."

The commodore chuckled. "I certainly can't say that I blame you," he said.

"It was quite a bust," Don admitted.

"Well," the commodore chuckled again. "I don't suppose we can throw you into the guardhouse for being A.W.O.L. in view of your recent decoration."

There was nothing to say to that.

"By the way," the commodore said, "I haven't had the opportunity to congratulate you on your Kraden. Everything seemed to move so fast, I never got around to it. That was quite a feat, Colonel."

"Thank you, sir," Don said. He added modestly, "Rather foolish of me, I suppose."

"Very much so, as everyone in Space Command has said. On such foolishness, however, are heroic deeds based, Colonel." The commodore looked at him questioningly. "You undoubtedly had incredible luck. The only way we've been able to figure it was that his detectors, his sensors, were on the blink. Do you think that is what might have happened?"

"Yes, sir," Don nodded quickly. "That's the way I figure it. And my first beaming must have disrupted his fire control, or whatever the equivalent to it is on Kraden cruisers. It was all a fluke."

The commodore said, "He didn't get in any return fire at all?"

"That's the damnedest thing about it. I'm not really sure, possibly a few blasts. But by that time I was in too close and moving too fast. The fact of the matter is, sir, I don't think they ever recovered from my first beaming of them. That's the only way I can account for them not blasting me into molecules. All I would have taken was one minor hit."

"That's probably it, all right," the commodore said musingly. "It's a shame you had to burn them so badly. We've never recovered a Kraden ship in good enough shape to give our techs something to work on. It might make a basic difference in the war, particularly if there was something aboard that we could decipher that would give us some indication of where they were coming from and how they get back and forth at the speed involved. We've been fighting this war for half a century—in our own backyard. It would help if we could get into *their* backyard for a change. It's problematical how long we can hold them off at this rate. If they ever come through with another major fleet, like they did the first time, or, more likely, even a larger fleet. . . ."

Don Mathers said uncomfortably, "Well, it's not as bad as all that, sir. We've held them thus far."

His superior grunted. "We've probably held them thus far because we've been able to keep out enough patrols to give us ample warning when one of their ships sneaks through. Do you know how much fuel that consumes, Colonel? How much uranium?"

"Well, I know it's a lot," Don told him, very seriously, very earnestly. "I've been studying up on it lately."

The other nodded wearily. "So much so that Earth's industry is switching back to petroleum and coal. Every ounce of radioactives is needed by the Space Service. Even so, it's just a matter of time."

Don Mathers pursed his lips. "I didn't know it

was that bad. How is the work on nuclear fusion progressing? As far back as when I was a boy they were predicting a breakthrough any day."

A puzzled frown came over the small man's face. He said, "Somehow or other the whole project seems under a hex. Accidents are continually happening; key scientists die, or become incapacitated for one reason or the other. One of our top physicists, a Hungarian chap, just disappeared. If we could just develop nuclear fusion, all our radioactives problems would be over." He chuckled sourly. "And overnight all those artificial settlements on the satellites would become ghost towns."

A cold, suspicious finger traced its way up the spine of Don Mathers.

The commodore said, "I'm afraid I'm being a wet blanket thrown over your big binge of a celebration, Colonel. Tell me, how does it feel to hold the system's highest award?"

Don shook his head, marveling. "Fantastic, sir. Of course, like any member of the Space Service I've always known of the Galactic Medal of Honor, but . . . well, nobody ever expects to get it." He added, with a short laugh, "Certainly not while he's still alive and in good health. Why, sir, do you realize that for all practical purposes I haven't been able to spend one pseudo-dollar of my credit since?" There was an element of awe in his voice. "Sir, do you realize that not even a beggar will accept anything from me?"

The commodore nodded in appreciation. "You must understand the unique position you occupy, Colonel. Your feat was inspiring enough, but that's not all of it. In a way, you combine both a popular hero with an *Unknown Soldier* element. Awarding you the Galactic Medal of Honor makes a symbol of you, a symbol representing all the thousands of unsung heroes and heroines who have died or been disabled in our space effort. It's not a light burden to carry on your shoulders, Colonel Mathers. I would imagine it a very humbling honor."

"Well, yes, sir," Don said.

The commodore twisted in a movement of embarrassment, and said, "It is with apology that I confess I had completely misjudged you . . . Donal. Very frankly, I thought you a cop-out, after that second to the last patrol of yours. You have amply proven how wrong I was."

Don played it very sincere. "I don't blame you, sir," he said. "In fact, to some extent you were correct. I was beginning to decide that you were right, that I should be psyched."

"You proved otherwise," Bernklau said and then switched his tone of voice. "That brings us to the present and what your next assignment is to be. Obviously, it wouldn't do for you to continue in a One Man Scout, particularly with your present rank. Space Command seems to be in favor of using you for morale projects and——"

191

Don Mathers cleared his throat and interrupted. "Sir, I've decided to drop out of the Space Service."

"Drop out!" The other stared at him, uncomprehendingly. "We're at war, Colonel!"

Don nodded seriously. "Yes, sir. And what you just said is true. I couldn't be used any longer in a One Man Scout, and I don't have the background to command a larger vessel. I'd wind up selling bonds and giving talks to old ladies' clubs."

"Well, hardly that, Colonel."

"No, sir. I think I'll be of more use out of the services. I'm tendering my resignation and making arrangements to help in the developing of Callisto and the other Jupiter satellites."

The commodore said nothing. His lips seemed to be whiter than before.

Don Mathers said doggedly, "Perhaps my prestige will help bring in volunteers to work the new mines out there. If they see me, well, sacrificing, putting up with all of the hardships. . . ."

The commodore said evenly, "Mr. Mathers, I doubt if you will ever have to put up with hardships again, no matter where you make your abode. However, good luck. You deserve it."

XIII

Inwardly laughing, Don Mathers made his way out of the building. He would never forget the way the commodore's eyes popped when he announced that he was dropping out of the Space Service. Had he made such an announcement a month ago, he would have been dropped all right, all right, right into the laps of a bunch of psych doctors' laps. But now? Now there was absolutely nothing the brass could do. He was out! At long last, he was out! No more three week patrols in deep space. No more space cafard. No more toadying to officers who ranked him. No more scorn to be seen in the eyes of his chief mechanic when he came in prematurely from an aborted patrol.

No more of the damned military, period!

He got his full salute at the entrance to the administration buildings again and stood there for a moment on the curb, waiting for the hovercart he summoned on his transceiver. While he waited, half a dozen passing officers stopped to shake hands and congratulate him. He recognized several of them, but none too well. They were all of different squadrons than his own. However, the way they gushed, you would have thought they were lifelong buddies. It was a relief when the hovercart pulled up and he got into it.

He dialed the living quarters of the Third Division and got out before the non-residents' dressing rooms. On his way over he'd had to answer to a few score waves of passers-by who recognized him. All right, it was part of the game and to be truthful it gave him a bit of ego-boo.

He made his way to his locker and opened it. He had been away only a couple of weeks or so, but already the contents looked foreign to him, as though he had never seen them before.

He brought out the several personal things that he wanted to retain, but left most of the locker's contents where they were. Anybody who wanted them could scrounge them. Probably quite a few would want to, as souvenirs of such a celebrity.

He undressed, threw the colonel's uniform aside, and brought forth the civilian suit he customarily kept in the locker. If he had anything to say about it, that was the last time he'd ever be seen in a uniform. The civilian suit was a bit on the proletarian side, he recognized now, but he could remedy that as soon as he got to an order box. From now on, Don Mathers was yearly going to make the Ten Best Dressed Men of the Solar System list.

Then, even as he redressed, something either
Demming or Rostoff said came back to him. They
were going to sponsor a "simplicity look" with some
far-out plan in mind to lower the standard of living,
and with it wage and salary standards. Well, he
could think about that later.

Among the things in his locker had been his wrist
chronometer, which he had never taken with him
into space. For one thing, there was a chronometer
in the cockpit of his V-102, and secondly he didn't
want to run the risk of batting it against something
while in free fall.

He took it up now and sneered slightly as he compared it to the one that had been given him in Geneva.

There was an enlisted man nearby, idly supervis-
ing a half a dozen automatic floor waxers. Don
called him over and proffered the chronometer.

"Could you use this, spaceman? I don't need it
any more."

The other goggled. "Your own personal wrist
chronometer?"

Don said impatiently, "Yes, of course. I have a
new one. Take it if you want it."

The other all but grabbed in his anxiousness. He
blurted, "Almighty Ultimate! Imagine! I'll be able
to show it to my grandkids and tell them it was the
chronometer of Colonel Donal Mathers and he
gave it to me personally!"

Don remembered that the German girl had said

195

something similar. She was going to be able to tell her grandchildren that she was the first woman Don had laid after winning his fight over the Kraden—while she was on her honeymoon.

He'd had a small bag in his locker. He put his things into it and left.

He summoned another hovercart and dialed the entrance of the base, but the screen of the small vehicle said, the computer voice metallic, "This transportation is restricted to space base personnel."

Don said laconically, "I am Colonel Donal Mathers."

"Yes, sir. Apologies." The hovercart took off.

At the entry of the base, the guard sprang to attention, but Don ignored them. So far as he was concerned, if he never gave or received a salute again, it would still be too soon.

He dismissed the cart and summoned a hovercab and, after a moment's hesitation, dialed Harry Amanroder's Nuevo Mexico Bar. It wasn't, of course, very far. He could have walked it. However, he'd just as well not be spotted. He'd wind up leading a host into the bar and spend his time there shaking hands and writing autographs.

At least, he was less conspicuous in civvies. He brought out his Universal Credit Card when they arrived at the bar and put it in the slot. The cab's screen voice said, "Company's orders. The credit card of Colonel Mathers is not to be recognized."

He assumed that meant he wasn't expected to

pay. He got out of the cab and hustled into the bar, wanting to get off the street before being spotted.

At this time of the morning, there was only one customer present, a Space Service lieutenant sitting on a stool at the bar. Harry Amanroder, of course, presided, and was idly wiping the space before him with a soiled bar rag. His pudding face broke when he saw who the newcomer was.

"Lootenant . . . I mean, Colonel Mathers! I . . . I never expected to see you ever come in this dump again!"

Don took a stool, two down from the lieutenant, and said, smiling, "This is my favorite bar, Harry. Besides, I have a tab here that's been accumulating for months. Hell, for all I know, for years."

Harry stood before him, tears in his eyes. "No, sir. That tab's been picked up."

Don scowled at him. "By whom?"

"By me."

Don shook his head. "No, sir, Harry. A hundred times you've put my guzzle on the cuff when I was broke. I've got more credits in my account than I've ever had before, and I'm having no luck at all spending them. But I'm going to pay your bill. I'll consider it a special favor, if you'll let me."

Harry said, his voice all but breaking, "All right, sir. But from then on in, the same thing applies in this bar as anywhere else in the Solar System. A holder of the Galactic Medal of Honor doesn't pay no tab."

"All right," Don said, in acceptance of the inevitable. "But let me have my accounting." He stuck his Universal Credit Card into the payment slot before him.

Harry went and got the bill from a sheaf of bills in a confusion of fellow bills in a drawer. Don wondered how in the hell the man stayed in business when he wouldn't turn down the credit requests of any man in space uniform.

Actually, Don was surprised at the magnitude of his own. Hadn't he *ever* paid up even part of his bar tab? Not that he gave a damn. He made the credit transfer and then said, "How about a tequila, for old time's sake, Harry? I haven't had a tequila since I was in here last."

The lieutenant down the bar from him said, in a woozy voice, "How about one with me, Don?"

It was Eric Hansen, who had been here the last time Don had dropped by. A fellow One Man Scout pilot and a member of Don's squadron—Don's former squadron, he amended thankfully. Eric was already obviously drenched. At this time of the morning? He was asking for it. It wouldn't be long before he was ordered psyched, if he wanted it or not.

"Sure, Eric," Don said.

The other slid off his stool and climbed shakily up on the one next to Don Mathers.

Harry said worriedly, "You sure you need any

more, Lootenant Hansen? Dint you tell me you were
due to go on patrol today?"

"Shut up," Eric said. "That's why I need another
one. I'll have a tequila, too, though why I should
drink that rotgut is a holy mystery. How's it going,
Don, you lucky son-of-a-bitch?"

Don said, a little irritated, "I didn't ask for the
damn decoration."

"That's not what I was talking about. I mean
you're lucky to be alive."

"That I am," Don admitted, going into his usual
modesty routine. "But anybody else would have
done the same thing."

"Go up against a Miro Class cruiser? Like hell I
would. I would have hung back out of range on his
flanks as long as I could keep him in my sensors
and reported to Command. In fact, that's exactly
what I did do when I spotted mine."

Don said uncomfortably, "You didn't have time
to close in. You hardly more than glimpsed yours."

"Thank the Almighty Ultimate I only glimpsed
him," Eric slurred. "I nearly shit myself as it was."

Don ignored that. He took up his salt and tequila
and toasted the other. "Cheers, cheers," he said.

They went through the tequila ceremony and
Eric Hansen reeled to the point Don was afraid he'd
fall off the stool. Harry looked at him worriedly.

He said to Don, "Won't they throw him into the
brig?"

199

Don said, trying to keep bitterness from his voice, in his new role as hero, "No. They'll throw him into space, with an initial double dose of oxygen. He'll sober up out there. What percentage of Scouts do you think go up completely drenched?"

Harry didn't answer that, but he looked distressed.

Eric said, "You wanta know something, Don?"

"Sure, Eric."

"Well, you know that last time I saw you you asked if I really saw that Kraden I reported that time? You told me about that friend of yours who didn't think they were really coming back. And you know, I got around to believing that he was right. I had a touch of cafard, knock on wood . . ." he knocked on the bar which wasn't wood but plastic ". . . and just imagined it. But now I know I was wrong. If you knocked one of them out, they're still coming back."

Don couldn't think of anything to say.

Eric looked at his chronometer and slurred, "I gotta be getting over to the base. Listen, Don, what are you doing in mufti?"

"I just resigned."

"I wish the hell I could," Eric Hansen said, slipping from his stool. He looked about the bar, his eyes finally coming to rest on the two tired potted cactus plants flanking the door. "Well, *adios*, guys. Isn't that what they say in Mexico?"

Neither Don nor Harry knew what they said in Mexico.

They watched the space pilot stumble toward the entrance.

"He drinks too much," Harry said worriedly. "Don't you guys have to be sharp all the time out in deep space?"

"Not for a day or so," Don told him. "It's all pretty automated at first. Not until you get to your own patrol sector." He was sorry now he had come here.

Eric Hansen had hardly left before the door swung open again and a king-sized redhead entered. Both Don and the bartender looked up.

In surprise, Don recognized the newcomer. What in the hell was his name? Thor, something or other. The big man had rescued him from the drunken footpads and then took him back to his apartment to sleep off his own load of guzzle. It came back to Don Mathers. A present-day pacifist who didn't believe in the all out effort against the Kradens.

The overgrown viking came up with a grin on his square face. He held out a hand and said, "Thor Bjornsen. Remember me?"

Don shook and said, "Sure I remember you. You saved my neck. What in the world are you doing here?"

The other looked around the barroom, noting it was empty, and spotting a booth in the furthest corner. "Looking for you," he said. "Could I have a few minutes of your time?"

"You can have all of my time you want. How about a drink?"

"Okay. Let's go over to that booth. I'd like to keep it private."

They ordered their drinks and carried them over to the booth and got in it across from each other.

Don said, "How'd you know I was in here?"

Thor Bjornsen told him, "It was on the news this morning that you had returned to Center City. I remembered that you'd made it rather clear that you didn't like the Space Service. I made an educated guess that one of the first things you'd do is come out here and resign." He took in the civilian suit Don was wearing. "Was I right?"

"Yes."

"At any rate, I came out and hung around the main entrance to the base. Finally, I spotted you leaving and followed you over here."

Don took a swallow of his drink and scowled at the other. The drink tasted awful after the guzzle he'd been drinking recently. "Why?" he said.

"I wanted to talk to you about that Kraden you destroyed. You see, you flushing the cruiser and shooting it out with him throws the whole argument of the organization I belong to out of kilter."

"How do you mean?" Don said cautiously.

"Remember? Our story is that the Kradens aren't coming back. They were a peaceful armada, probably interested in trade, or new planets to colonize, if they weren't already occupied."

Don said grumpily, "That big shoot-out we had with them half a century ago didn't indicate that they were exactly peace lovers."

The big man was unhappy at that. He said slowly, "As I mentioned to you before, some of us aren't sure that the Kradens participated in that shoot-out. That possibly they were shocked by the attack upon them and simply disappeared back into hyperspace, or whatever they call it."

Don said, "Look, even if they were originally peacefully inclined, once our four space fleets hit them, they'd fire back."

The big Scandinavian shook his head. "Not necessarily. The human race doesn't subscribe to Jesus' teaching that, if someone slaps you, turn the other cheek. But that doesn't mean that more advanced, more enlightened cultures might not believe in it. Possibly when attacked, and even after having lost some of their spaceships, the Kradens, with their higher ethics, simply left."

"Why did my cruiser come back?"

"How do you know it was a cruiser? Perhaps it was a merchantman, an explorer, possibly it was a ship bearing ambassadors." Thor leaned forward. "Tell me the truth, Don. Did it fire at you? Even after you had initiated your attack?"

Don ran his tongue over his lip. He liked this man and was in his debt. However, there was nothing he could do without risking his neck. He said, finally, "Frankly, I can't be sure. I was all caught up in the excitement, moving as fast as I could."

Thor slumped back in his seat. He thought about it. He said finally, "Very possibly the Kradens were sending out another peaceful feeler to us. After the lapse of fifty years, perhaps their hope was that our warlike attitude toward extraterrestrials had cooled."

"Perhaps," Don said, putting doubt in his voice.

"It can never be proven now," the other said in disgust. He finished his drink. "What are you going to do now that you're a civilian again? I would have thought you might stay in and get some chairborne assignment that would keep you out of space but still allow you to enjoy your prestige."

"I don't have to wear a uniform to enjoy my prestige, as you put it. In fact, I'm beginning to wish I could avoid some of the damn prestige. But at any rate, I'm going to throw myself all out into the war effort to exploit the radioactives on the satellites."

Thor stared at him. "They're exploiting them too damn much as it is. In ten years there won't be any remaining. If we haven't solved the nuclear fusion problem by then there simply won't be any radioactives left."

Don Mathers couldn't think of anything to say to that. If anything, he'd welcome the day. It would free him of Demming and Rostoff. They wouldn't have any need of him any longer.

His companion waved at Harry to bring them a refill and then went into it. He said, "We're destroying ourselves in destroying the solar system's raw materials like this. It's an utterly mad socioeconomic system. Are you at all up on economic history?"

"No," Don said. What's more, he couldn't care less.

"Well, the last century in particular has been chaotic. Unbelievable. Classical capitalism, of the type raged against by Marx, actually collapsed in 1929. And never recovered. After ten years of economic chaos, prosperity was restored by the Second World War. The resources, both material and labor power, of practically the whole world were thrown into the military effort. Business boomed. When the war ended, so had classical capitalism. A form of what some call State Capitalism took over. The State entered into the economy to the point of dominating it. The military-industrial complex took over, increasingly, supported by government. Supposed prosperity was maintained by spending endless billions on the military. Supposedly the West and East were confronting each other eyeball to eyeball but in actuality their basic socioeconomic systems had little real difference. The Soviet Complex called itself communist, or socialist, but in truth, it was simply a different version of State Capitalism. The major difference was that instead of having individual capitalists and corporations owning the means of production, they were owned by the State, headed by the Communist parties whose heads profited by the system. But basically both Eastern and Western economies were systems of waste, destruction of natural resources, pollution, inflation, threatened collapse of the international monetary system, overproduction in the developed countries and under-production in the undeveloped. These along with the uncontrolled population explosion were leading to a complete collapse. Only the coming of the Kradens prevented it. It was a shot in the arm, somewhat similar to the Second World War. Overnight, the planet was united and became an armed camp. The space program boomed, colonies went to every planet and satellite in the system that could support human life. Unemployment ceased to exist, production boomed."

Don said, wearying of the long harangue, "Well, isn't that for the good? At least nobody starves anymore. Everybody has work."

Thor looked at him pityingly. "For how long? We're ripping off not only the resources of Earth but now of the whole solar system. Ninety percent of the efforts are going into space and so-called defense. How long before we've stripped ourselves naked?"

Don had never thought about it. And he still didn't give a damn. He had his and would continue to have it for the rest of his life. If what Thor said was correct, let the powers that be figure it out when the time came. After him the deluge? Okay, let it rain.

XIV

Harry came up hesitantly, a camera in his heavy freckled hands and said "Colonel Mathers, I bought me this here Tri-Di camera on the off-chance you might come by again some day. I wanted to get a shot of you, here in my bar, so I could frame it and hang it on the wall and people'd know you usta hang out here before you got famous."

"Sure, Harry," Don said, standing. "Where do you want me?"

"How about up against the bar?"

Thor stood too and said, "Why not let me take it? You get behind the bar, uh, Harry. And let Don get in front of it. Then you'll both be in the shot."

Harry radiated at that. "You don't mind, Colonel Mathers?"

"Of course not."

Thor Bjornsen took three pictures in all, from different angles, and then he and Don went back to the booth.

The Scandinavian looked at him. "Do you get much of that sort of thing?"

"Yes."

Thor said, "To get back to the radioactives thing. Who's in it with you?"

Don wondered whether or not to answer, but, after all, it would probably soon be in the news. He said, "Lawrence Demming and Maximilian Rostoff, who already have large investments in the field and plenty of know-how, are putting up the initial capital to get going."

The other took him in in horror. "Demming and Rostoff? They're the two biggest crooks in the system."

"I'm to be president of the corporation. I'll keep them in line."

"What do you get out of it, Don?"

"Nothing. Nothing except my expenses."

Thor Bjornsen frowned. "And nobody else is in it at all?"

"Well, actually, Peter Fodor has been given a chunk of stock. He's going to throw the weight of the Church behind the, uh, crusade."

"Almighty Ultimate! If Demming and Rostoff are the two biggest crooks in the system, he's the third."

"What are you talking about? He's the Grand Presbyter."

"Yes, and like most big organized religions down through the centuries, his church is a racket, with him the chief racketeer. Religions might start humbly with the leaders really living up to their vows of poverty and so forth—take Christ and his apostles and early followers. They lived in a sort of primitive communism. But have you ever read an account of the church at the time of the Borgias and the Medici? When you get to the top of the heap in business, you don't become a multi-millionaire by remaining honest. When you get to the top in politics, it isn't by keeping your hands clean."

"I'm not up on politics," Don admitted.

"Well," the other said. "My point was that big business, such as Demming's and Rostoff's type, big politics, and even big religion are headed by corrupt men—since power corrupts."

Don was getting tired of it. He had made his decision and there was no way to back out of it, even if he had wanted to, and he didn't.

He looked at his wrist chronometer and said, "Sorry, Thor, I'm going to have to get underway."

The other nodded unhappily. "All right, Don. But think about what I've said. The human race is bleeding the system white with all this so-called defense preparation. If you'd throw your prestige onto the scales, you'd be able to counter this industrial-military-political combine that's now in control."

Don stood and said, "I'll think about it, Thor."

He headed for the door, calling over his shoulder, "So long, Harry. Thanks for the drinks."

The bartender looked after him, wistfully, worshipfully.

Thor came up, pulling his Universal Credit Card from an inner pocket. He said, "How much do I owe you?"

Harry looked at him indignantly. "No man who's been drinking with Colonel Donal Mathers pays in this bar."

"Oh, excuse me," the big fellow said, trying to keep sarcasm from his voice.

Don had little difficulty in getting back to Demming's place. He didn't make the mistake of going in the front entrance of the building, strongly suspecting that there'd be a multitude of media people there. Instead, he had dialed the hovercab for the motor pool area in the basements. He got the cab as near as possible to Demming's private elevator bank before getting out and strolling rapidly toward the nearest one. He was stopped only twice for handshakes and gushing congratulations.

His intention had been to go directly to Rostoff's office but when he left the elevator he was halted in his tracks for a moment.

In the huge foyer a magnificent sign had been raised. DONAL MATHERS RADIOACTIVES MINING CORPORATION.

Evidently, he decided, the new corporation had taken over this entire floor. Things were moving. One thing you had to give his two partners, Demming and Rostoff, they didn't drag their heels.

Actually, he hadn't as yet been able to come to definite conclusions about the position he was in.

He was being used by the two magnates, but he couldn't figure any way of getting out from under. However, he was also aware of the fact that they couldn't twist his arm too much. They needed him a damn sight more than he needed them. In fact, nothing would please him more than if they'd both drop dead.

He reached Rostoff's office, after wading through an ocean of smiles from office personnel, and was immediately passed through by the worshipful receptionist.

Rostoff was alone. He looked up at Don's entrance.

"Where the hell have you been, you damned rummy? I can smell your breath from here."

It was still difficult for Don Mathers to adjust himself to his sudden change in status, whenever he was alone with either of his two supposed partners. When among others, he was treated like a semigod. When alone with Demming or Rostoff, he was treated like a peasant.

He said, "I've been resigning from the Space Service.

"Good," Maximilian Rostoff said. He took in Don's suit. "I see you've already adopted the simplicity look. Your suit looks as though you earn about seventy-five pseudo-dollars a week."

Don sighed and took a chair. "It's the only suit I had in my locker at the base."

"Well, keep wearing that type of clothing whenever you're in public."

Don hesitated before saying, "There's something you probably ought to know. On the way over to the base, Frank Cockney tried to pump me."

Rostoff was suddenly alert, eyes narrowed. "What do you mean? Exactly what did he say?"

"I can't remember the exact words, but he thought it quite a coincidence that you and Demming had sent for me just previous to my knocking out the Kraden, and then immediately after my award, you getting together with me again and the corporation being formed. In fact, I got the feeling that he knew the corporation was already being formed *before* I got my medal."

"Who else was there?"

"His sidekick, Bil Golenpaul."

"What did he say?"

"Nothing."

"But he heard the whole conversation?"

"That's right."

"What did you say?"

"I clammed up."

"All right. I'll take care of it. Come on." The tycoon got up and headed for the office room's elevator.

"Come on where?" he said now, following the other.

They got into the compartment and Rostoff gave the screen orders. Then he said to Don, "We've got a

212

half dozen speech writers for you and a couple of coaches. They're going to make you the best public speaker since William Jennings Bryan."

Don had never heard of Bryan. He said, "Six speech writers? Why so many?"

"One is actually the head of your public relations staff. Each is a specialist in some field. One in radio-actives, one on the Jupiter satellites, one in religion, one in corporation law, and so forth. Every time you open your trap, the words that come out will indicate you're one of the most erudite men in the system."

The internal transport system of this portion of the Interplanetary Lines Building—call it an elevator if you will—took them this way and that and finally up to the next floor. They stopped, the door opened and they emerged into a moderately-sized conference room. There were nine men seated around the heavy table, coffee or drinks before them. One of them was Dirck Bosch, Demming's secretary. The others Don didn't recognize.

He took that back. He did recognize two of them. They were top Tri-Di actors. They were both sympathetic, he-man types, both in Don's age group and both approximately his own size.

All came to their feet when Don and Rostoff entered, and all gathered around to be introduced and to congratulate the hero. The whole group of sophisticates were as gushing as the crowds that gathered whenever he got into public. He

213

didn't catch any of their names, save those of the two actors, and he knew them already, of course; Ken Westley and Rexford Lucas. It came as a shock to realize that both were homosexuals, and neither bothered to disguise the fact off-lens as they were now. Both even had limp handshakes and he suspected that both would like to get him into bed.

When they found seats again—Don being given the place of honor at the head of the table—Dirck looked at first at Rostoff and then quickly to Don. Don was inwardly amused, sourly. The Belgian was in on the whole secret but was going to have to continually remind himself that in public Don was the big cheese.

Dirck Bosch said, "I have been briefing these gentlemen on the whole project, stressing the fact that in the past Colonel Mathers was a space pilot, as we are all so admiringly aware, but that he is inexperienced in addressing the public."

"I'm afraid it's Mr. Mathers now, Dirck," Don said. "You see, in order that I would be able to devote full time to the corporation and its, uh, ideals, I resigned my commission this morning."

There was some surprise at that and a few raised eyebrows.

One of the writers said, "Ummm. Couldn't you have simply taken an indefinite leave of absence?"

But Maximilian Rostoff pursed his lips and put in, "No, I think Donal was correct. It will be more dramatic if he renounces his promotion and throws his whole weight into the defense preparations. However, I think it might be well to continue to call him Colonel in our press dispatches."

The wolfish looking tycoon turned to one of the other writers, the PR man, and said, "Mullens, when we get out a press release on this, you might stress the fact that the Colonel resigned his commission since he thought himself unworthy of such a rank at his age and with his lack of experience. He didn't choose to be a meaningless figurehead, in these pressing times."

"Right." The other made some quick notes on the pad before him.

One of the actors, Rexford Lucas said, "To get down to the nitty-gritty and gather some material on Don's style-to-be, I think at first we should have him walk about the room."

Rostoff looked at the space hero. "Do you mind, Don?"

More mystified than anything else, Don got up and walked around the room a couple of times.

"And just stand there for a moment, as though you were facing a microphone," Ken Westley said.

Don just stood there for a moment, looking back at them, and feeling like a damn fool.

"Make a gesture, as though you were trying to make a strong point," Westley said.

Don made a gesture, as though trying to cinch a point.

"Hmmm," Rexford Lucas said. "Have you ever

done any public speaking at all, or did you belong to the dramatic club, or take drama, when you were in school?"

"No."

"Didn't belong to the debating team or anything like that?"

"No, I didn't," Don said, and went back and sat down again.

All regarded him for a long silent moment.

Rexford Lucas said, "For one thing, I think we'd better have a still more military stance and walk. Very straight. The bearer of the Galactic Medal of Honor must walk tall."

One of the writers said to Don, "Let's hear you talk."

Don looked at him. "What should I say?"

"Anything. We just want to get a level on your speaking voice. Recite a poem, or something."

Don thought about that for a long moment. He said finally, "Back when I was a kid in school we had to memorize a poem called, *Daffodils.*"

"Daffodils!" Rostoff muttered.

"Anything'll do. Try it," the writer said.

Don cleared his throat and began.

I wandered lonely as a cloud
  That floats on high or dale and hill.
Uh, when all at once I saw a crowd,
  A host of, uh, golden daffodils,

Beside a lake, beneath the trees,
  Fluttering and dancing in the breeze.

The waves beside them danced, but they
  Outdid the sparkling waves in, uh, glee.
A poet could not be gay
  In such a jocund company.
I gazed and gazed, but, uh, little thought
  What wealth to me the show had brought

For oft when on my couch I lie,
  In vacant or in pensive mood,
They, uh, flash upon that inward eye,
  Which is the, uh, bliss of solitude.
And then my heart with pleasure fills
  And dances with the daffodils.

He wound up with, "I think there was one more stanza in there but I've forgotten it."

"Jesus," one of the writers said.

"I thought it was very sweet," Rexford Lucas simpered.

The writer who had asked him to recite sighed and looked over at Dirck Bosch. He said, "Look, could you get on the data banks screen and get a copy of the Gettysburg Address?"

They stuck to it for two hours or more and then

Rostoff and Don left the actors and speech writers to confer on what type of public speaker they were going to convert him into.

Most of them looked a little on the glum side. But Ken Westley waved him a limp wristed bye-bye.

Don and Rostoff got back into the elevator and the interplanetary magnate said, "You're beginning to get a sample of what you're in for. This afternoon you'll meet the writer who's going to turn out your autobiography. He's already studying your Dossier Complete."

"My Dossier Complete! Where'd you get it? Nobody's allowed to look at my dossier, unless it's an authorized official, with a court clearance."

Rostoff sighed. "You'll learn, you'll learn. Don't they have a saying in the military, that rank has its privileges? Well, believe me, they are as nothing to the privileges that wealth has."

"Damn it!" Don said in protest.

The other ignored him and said, "Demming is turning the whole penthouse over to you. It will be nice and secluded so you won't be molested by the mob. And it'll be a good place for doing your autobiography, news conferences, and business in general. You won't be bothered by anybody except rubbernecks trying to spot you from overflying aircraft. We'll assign a few heavies to you, to see that nobody gets through that you don't want to see, or we don't want to see you."

"Heavies?"

"Bodyguards."

"I don't need bodyguards. I'm the most popular man in the system."

"That you are, that you are," the other said with his lupine smile. "But in the near future you're going to be stepping on some toes. On top of that, there's always the crackpot. Anybody who shot Donal Mathers would go down in history. Oh, they'd catch him and probably execute him, even though he was as drivel-happy as a loon, but he'd go down in history."

The compartment stopped and they emerged into the living room of the oversized penthouse chalet.

Rostoff looked at him from the side of his eyes and said, "Are you sleeping with Alicia Demming?"

Don glowered back at him indignantly. "None of your goddamned business."

"Oh, but it is. Anything about you is my business. So far as Demming is concerned, he probably couldn't care less. His daughter has slept around before, probably ever since she was about twelve. I'm in favor of it. If you have a bedmate right here in the building, it'll keep you from prowling the town, looking for it."

"I don't have to look very hard," Don muttered.

"I'll bet you don't. Why don't you get yourself a drink? You look as though you could use one. Your ghost writer is in the library. I'll go get him. You can have a preliminary talk and then have lunch together."

"Where's Demming?"

"I think over in London. He'll probably be back by tomorrow."

Rostoff left and Don went over to the autobar. He dialed some of Demming's ancient Napoleon Brandy. He'd put a hole in that supply, he decided. The sonofabitch would be sorry he'd ever let Don Mathers loose in his fancy guzzle. He amended that. Don and his *friends*. He'd invite the gang up and there'd be some parties in this penthouse that would make history.

The cognac came and he knocked half of it back, before amending again. He suddenly realized that he, Donal Mathers, didn't have any real friends. The whole solar system loved him, but, now that he thought about it, he didn't have any real friends, just acquaintances. People like Eric Hansen? People like the space worshipping bartender, Harry? Nearer to it was Thor Bjornsen, whom he had met exactly twice.

XV

They gave him two full weeks of instructions and
rehearsals before clearing him for Tri-Di appear-
ances, news conferences, and making him available
to commentators and free lance writers for special
articles.

The people had begun to wonder where their new
hero was keeping himself; but Si Mullens, the PR
chief, and his staff of publicity men leaked just
enough material to placate them. For one thing, the
holder of the Galactic Medal of Honor was taking a
much needed rest after his soul-shattering, exhaust-
ing fight with the Kraden which had brought him
to the edge of nervous breakdown. For another,
Colonel Mathers was embarked upon a project
which he would soon reveal to the public, a project
even more important, and possibly as daring, as his
attack upon the Miro Class cruiser.

Meanwhile, Don stuck largely to the top floors of
the Interplanetary Lines Building. Occasionally,
he'd take a relaxing flight in one of the hover limou-

sines, invariably accompanied by two of the bodyguards. Except in the privacy of his penthouse quarters, and particularly in his own suite, he was never
out of sight of at least a couple of these and usually
more. They were supposedly secretaries of his but
all of them were professionals, armed with quick-
draw laser pistols. Even in the offices of the Donal
Mathers Radioactives Mining Corporation, they
were always present. Demming and Rostoff knew all
too well that if anything happened to their hero, the
whole project was a bust.

The offices were expanding and already took up
two floors of the building, and there were thousands
of employees, largely busily at work, sworn to se-
crecy about the soon to be revealed project.

Alicia came to his bed nightly and their relationship had become less frenetic, more easygoing. They
continued to enjoy each other sexually, but had
agreed that they would keep their affair quiet, not
even allowing the bodyguards to know of its existence. If word got out that Colonel Mathers had a
full time mistress, every newsman, every commen-
tator, every columnist, every photographer, every
news gossip in the system would be after her. Everything she had ever done would be dug into, and in
her time, Alicia told her lover wryly, she had done
quite a few things, usually hushed up by her father's influence, but nothing could be hushed up
pertaining to Don Mathers.

She surprised him one night, after they had finished making love, by saying, "My father has something on you, hasn't he, Don?"

He looked at her warily. "How do you mean?" He didn't like this. In the whole system, only Demming, Rostoff and Dirck Bosch knew. And even that was too damn many. It meant that for the rest of their lives he was under their thumbs. Even if the two older men died, he would still be at Bosch's mercy.

She said slowly, "I'm not stupid, Don. I've suspected it almost from the first. There's a something electric between you. There's a relationship between you and father and Max Rostoff that is particularly obvious when you're not in the vicinity of any outsiders."

"You're dreaming, darling. Our relationship is purely business."

"Yes, and with the preferred stock of the corporation, supposedly *your* corporation, the only stock that is going to count, in their hands."

"How did you know that?"

"I told you I wasn't stupid. The only one they've cut in at all, so far, is the Grand Presbyter. And only him because they want the weight of his Universal Reformed Church behind them."

Don sighed and said, "I don't need money, darling. And it looks good for me to be heading the corporation on a non-profit basis."

"What do you mean, you don't need money? Everybody needs money," she said in rejection.

He said, weariness there in his voice, "I suspect that if I called the largest bank on Earth and asked for a million pseudo-dollars, they'd give it to me on my signature."

"Ridiculous."

He said, "Watch this." He flicked on the phone screen that sat at the edge of the bed and dialed for his night secretary. When the other's face faded in, Don said, "Peters, what's the best automobile in the world?"

"Rolls-Royce Hover, Colonel."

"Very well, get me the head of their sales department. I don't give a damn what time it is, get him."

While he waited, Alicia said, "What's going on? We've got enough cars around here to carry a regiment."

He ignored her and surprisingly shortly, in view of the hour, another face replaced his secretary's. The newcomer was wide-eyed.

Don said, "I'm Colonel Donal Mathers and I'm considering buying one of your cars."

The other's jaw slipped. He stuttered, in a British accent, "Just . . . just a moment, ahh, Colonel. I'll put you in touch . . ." His voice dripped away and then his face faded, to be replaced in moments by another wide-eyed stranger.

This new one said, "I'm Gerald Hastings, sir. Head of Rolls-Royce Hover public relations. We'll immediately send you over a complete selection of all of our models."

Don said, "I don't think I could afford——"

The other was distressed. "Oh, sir, there would be no charge."

Don said, "I'll think it over. Thanks." He flicked off the other's distressed face before he could go into a sales pitch. Don knew what the other was thinking. The interplanetary hero was probably considering the vehicles of some of the competitors, Mercedes Hover, or whoever. He had a sneaking suspicion that the Rolls-Royce Hovers would be on the way to Center City before the night was out.

He turned to Alicia and said, "See what I mean? What would I do with money if I had it?"

She said, "Holy Almighty Ultimate, I didn't know it went *that* far."

"Well, it does. I can't spend a pseudo-cent. Hell, I can't give it away."

For the time, at least, they talked no more of the hold over Don that she sensed her father and Rostoff held.

She had never again mentioned the possibility of marriage. Don didn't know if it was because she had second thoughts, or if she was waiting for him to take the initiative. Actually, he still didn't know how he felt about it. She was a dish, but was she the kind of dish you'd want to spend the rest of your life with, even after the initial notoriety of his getting his medal had died away a bit and he was more able to appear in public places without being mobbed? That she was a spoiled, selfish young woman was obvious. But, on the other hand, one day she would inherit the Demming fortune and by that time the Demming fortune would be a damned sight larger than it was today. And although he didn't really need money now, perhaps the time would come. Money was power and he was beginning to like the feeling of power.

It was the day following this discourse with Alicia that the fourth man to join the holders of preferred stock came on the scene.

Don had been sitting at his desk, going over the speech he was to make the following day. This was only the second time he had been on Tri-Di lens and the first time, at the ceremony in Geneva, it wasn't a personal thing. He hadn't really given a speech or anything. He was unhappy about it, in spite of all the coaching the two actors had given him, and in spite of all the careful honing the speech writers had done to bring out the proper sincerity, the proper simplicity, the proper terminology. For instance, it wouldn't have done to use a single word or expression that couldn't be understood by everyone in the system older than ten.

The identity screen on the door buzzed and he flicked the button that activated it. Rostoff's face was there.

He said, oozing unctuousness, "May we come in, Colonel Mathers?"

Mildly surprised at the courtesy, Don flicked another button which opened the door.

Rostoff strode in, followed by a stranger, followed by Demming. All were fawning.

The stranger was a bluff, slightly red-faced type, who simply radiated good will and honesty. He was conservatively dressed, clear and deep of voice when he spoke. And in five seconds flat Don had branded him *politician.* The other could have gotten a job portraying a prominent politician any day in the week on Tri-Di.

Don began to stand but the newcomer said, still radiating cheerful admiration, "No, no, Colonel. Don't bother." He reached across the desk to shake hands. His grip was firm and friendly.

Demming wheezed, "Colonel Mathers, this is Senator Frank Makowski, of Callisto. Undoubtedly you have heard his inspired speeches over and over again; possibly when you were in deep space in your One Man Scout. He is Callisto's representative to the Solar System League's Parliament in Geneva."

"Yes, of course," Don said, smiling as best he could. He had never heard of the man in his life. "Please be seated, gentlemen. It's an honor to meet you personally, Senator."

The senator, even while finding his chair said, "Colonel Mathers, the honor is mine."

"Could I offer you gentlemen a drink?" Don said. He had already had two or three today, even though he was trying to concentrate on the speech.

Rostoff said, "No, no, Colonel. It's only four

o'clock and Lawrence and I are acquainted with your restrained drinking habits."

"Well," Don said, in deprecation, "I'm not exactly a teetotaler." The bastard. Don could have used another drink along in here.

"But almost," Demming said in his flat voice. "Colonel, we know how busy you are, but we have a business matter with the Senator, here, and in view of the fact that you are president and chairman of the board, he was desirous to clear it with you."

The senator chuckled. "In actuality, Colonel, my big motivation was to have the honor of meeting you. I have dealt with Mr. Demming and Mr. Rostoff before, in line of my duties, and, of course, trust them implicitly."

Don tried to look interested and sincere and held his peace.

Demming cleared his voice and said, "In view of the fact that Senator Makowski is in a key position so far as the corporation is concerned, it occurred to Max and me that possibly we should, ah, give him a piece of the action, as the old saying goes. He has invariably cooperated most generously with both Max and myself in earlier projects involving the mineral exploitation of Callisto and I am sure that in this more all out effort, his position will make it imperative that we work in full cooperation with him."

"Yes, indeed," Rostoff said.

"Of course, in this great crusade," the Senator

said, "you would have my all out support in any case——"

Don said, "What is the problem, gentlemen?" He hadn't the vaguest idea what they were talking about.

Rostoff said, "Lawrence and I have suggested that one percent of the preferred stock of the Donal Mathers Radioactives Mining Corporation be issued to the Senator."

Demming said, "And he wished your assurance that you completely concurred."

"Why, of course," Don said earnestly. "In fact, I had been considering bringing up the matter myself, except that I had thought in terms of two percent."

The Senator shone.

Demming and Rostoff glared.

Rostoff got out finally, "We shall have to look into it, Colonel Mathers. You are aware of how thinly stretched we already are." He came to his feet, followed by the other two. "I'll confer with you later on, after checking with the executive committee of the board."

When they were gone, Don snorted in both self-satisfaction and ill humor. He said aloud, "If they keep on passing out chunks of their stock to every crook who comes along with his hand extended, they'll be running out themselves, the bastards." He had to laugh at the expression on Rostoff's face as the three had filed out. The other was going to hit

the ceiling the next time he saw Don Mathers. Don
didn't give a damn.

They held the initial broadcast in a comparatively
small conference room of the offices of the corporation. The penthouse was too luxurious to fit in with
the soon to be mounted campaign for the Simplicity
Look. In fact, the conference room itself had been
redecorated with a less ostentatious table, less ornate chairs.

Don was alone save for Dirck Bosch and two of
the bodyguards, but these sat to one side, so as not
to appear on lens. The bodyguards kept their cold
eyes roaming continuously over the swarm of Tri-
Di technicians, in spite of the fact that all of these
had been electronically frisked as they entered the
building.

The director finally checked his wrist chronometer, turned and said to Don, "All ready, Colonel?"

"Ready as I'll ever be, I suppose," Don said.

The crew all laughed. Hell it wasn't as good a
bon mot as all that. It was just that he was Colonel
Mathers—modest attainer of the Galactic Medal of
Honor—and anything he said in self-deprecation
was humor.

Don, seated at the end of the table, looked down
at the speech. At first his coaches had wanted him
to memorize it and seem to be speaking off the cuff.
It would add to the utter sincerity which was the
big ingredient. But Don had killed that, telling them

that there wasn't a chance in the world of his being able to memorize anything as long as this. Besides, if he did it once, from then on every audience he addressed was going to expect it, and Don Mathers was scheduled for a lot of audiences in the near future.

The director pointed a finger at one of the cameras and counted down, one, two, three. A red light went on, indicating the conference room was hot. The director then, spoke, being on lens.

He said simply, "Fellow citizens of the Solar System League, I bring you Colonel Donal Mathers, sole living holder of the Galactic Medal of Honor. Colonel Mathers." He pointed his finger at Don dramatically, and another camera picked Don up, all three lenses shining at him.

Don looked up directly into them and went into his routine, the routine he had practiced so much with his two coaches.

He said, slowly and distinctly, "The project at hand is the extraction of the radioactives, the ores on the Jupiter satellites and perhaps the Saturn satellite, Titan. This endeavor is the highest top priority in the defense program."

He paused impressively before continuing.

"It is a job that cannot be done in slipshod, haphazard manner. The system's need for radioactives cannot be overstressed.

"In short, fellow humans, we must allow nothing

to stand in the way of all out, unified, effort to do this job quickly and efficiently. My associates and I have formed a corporation to manage this crash program. We invite all to participate by purchasing stock. I will not speak of profits, fellow humans, because in this emergency we all scorn them. However, as I say, you are invited to participate.

"Some of the preliminary mining concessions are at present in the hands of individuals or small corporations. It will be necessary that these turn over their holdings to our single all-embracing organization for the sake of efficiency. Our experts will evaluate such holdings and recompense the owners."

Don Mathers paused again for emphasis.

"This is no time for quibbling. All must come in. If there are those who put private gain before the needs of the system, then pressures must be found to be exerted against them. Public opinion will not allow them to profit while the fate of the Solar System is in the balance.

"We will need thousands and tens of thousands of trained workers to operate our mines, our mills, our refineries. In the past, skilled labor on the satellites was used to double or triple the wage rates on Earth. I need only repeat, this is no time for personal gain and quibbling. The corporation announces proudly that it will pay only prevailing Earth rates. We will not insult our employees by 'bribing' them to patriotism through higher wages."

There was more, along the same lines.

232

It was all taken very well. Indeed, it was taken with universal enthusiasm.

Si Mullens leaked the fact that the interplanetary hero was taking no salary whatsoever for his contributions.

XVI

Don Mathers spent the next weeks, the next months, in what was seemingly a chaos of interviews, speeches and press releases, though many of the last he never saw. The efficient Si Mullens turned them out wholesale, and was more apt to check them, before release, with Demming or Rostoff rather than Don.

Actually, Rostoff and Demming remained in the background. They never allowed themselves to be seen in Don's company in public, or even when news people were around. They went to considerable effort and expense to suppress any news stories about their being affiliated with the corporation. It wasn't as hard as all that to do. Between the two of them, they had large financial interests in most of the important media. Those news outlets which they didn't personally control, largely belonged to fellow members of the financial elite who owed them favors, or possibly not adverse to accumulating some credit with the two men who had already become the wealthiest magnates in the system. No matter what field you were in, it was most likely that sooner or later you'd have some reason to call upon Demming and/or Rostoff.

It wouldn't have been so bad, perhaps, if he could have spent more of his time in a haze of alcohol, but his binges were restricted to after-hours. He had to maintain his Boy Scout image. Supposedly, he didn't drink, he didn't smoke, and the sighing matrons, un-weds and virgins of the solar system could go to bed at night and dream of marrying—or at least having an affair with—Don Mathers. He was a bachelor. The secret of Alicia was as well kept as that of Eva Braun and her relationship with Hitler.

It wasn't all strawberries and cream by a long shot.

A couple of months after the initial announcement, he was politely invited to Demming's office, his innermost, most private, sanctum sanctorum.

There Sam Frankle was introduced. Don was aware of him, though not in any detail. President of the One Big Union. Once a common copper miner, he had evidently fought his way up through union politics—sometimes with his heavy, merciless fists. He was bettle-browed, broken-nosed, and there were obvious scars on his dark face. In this age of plastic surgery, Don wondered? He supposed it was part of the other's image. He was extremely popular with the workers he led, supposedly continuously fighting for their rights.

Frankle took the space hero in, his eyes less than friendly. He was not the hero worshipping type, obviously.

Present were Demming, Rostoff and the unassuming Dirck Bosch, and all three were empty of face.

Don said, after becoming properly seated, "What can I do for you, Mr. Frankle?"

"They call me Bull Frankle, and I want to know what the shit's going on."

Don looked from Demming to Rostoff and could tell nothing from their expressions, although both were alert of eye. He looked back at the union leader. "I don't believe I follow you, ah, Bull."

The tough man said, "Look, Mr. Interplanetary Hero, let me tell you some of the facts of life. Unions are big business. Like any other kind of big business they exist to make money for the people who own, or control them. For instance, Lawrence Demming's Interplanetary Conglomerate doesn't exist for the people who work in it, several hundred thousands. It exists for him."

"Get to the point, Bull," Rostoff said.

"That is the point. I want to know my *in*." He looked at Don suspiciously. "You made a big talk to the marks, the suckers. Everybody's got to sacrifice, including the workers on Callisto and so forth, all members of the One Big Union. Okay, some of them will take it. Most of them will take it. You say they shouldn't get double wages, on account of working on the satellites. Okay, you want to know something? If they don't get anything extra, as a result of the union being in there pitching for them, why should they keep membership in the union and pay out their dues?"

"I'm not up on all this," Don said weakly. He didn't know what it was all about.

"That's why I'm briefing you," the other said impatiently. "I know you're not up on it. But you're asking these funkers to work at Earth-side pay, when things are such up there they can't even bring their families up, most of them, and it's pretty damn slim living and it's a damn sight more dangerous than working on Earth. Okay. So what is it the One Big Union is going to do for them? From what you say, nothing."

Don looked at his two supposed partners.

Demming said flatly, "We must all sacrifice together in these times."

Bull Frankle didn't even bother to laugh. "I want in," he said. "And I also have to have something to throw my boys, otherwise they drop out of the organization. Don't you characters get the point? Everybody's got to get something, or they start looking somewheres else. Now what can I promise my boys, so they'll want to stay in the union?"

"And so that you can continue milking them of dues," Rostoff said, thinking it out.

"Okay, put it that way if you wanta get on a snotty level. I thought we was all practical men around here."

"Don't misunderstand," Demming wheezed thoughtfully. "You make the problem clear. Hmmm. Max?"

Maximilian Rostoff said, "How about this? As a result of the efforts of Samuel Frankle, President of the One Big Union, the government of the Solar System League has ruled that any worker on any planet or satellite off Earth shall receive two year's credit toward any pensions, social security, that sort of thing, for each year he spends off Earth. A very patriotic step, highly endorsed by the bearer of the Galactic Medal of Honor. All this through the efforts of the One Big Union, and, frankly, costing our corporation not one extra pseudo-cent."

Demming and Frankle looked at him in admiration.

Frankle said, "Okay, that seems to cover that part of it, if you can swing it, and, through Mathers, here, I assume you can. Now, where's my in?"

Don wasn't following too well. He wished that he could get a double shot of something or other. But he said, "What in?"

Frankle looked at him as though he was completely around the corner.

"My *in*, my *in*." He was exasperated. "What do I get out of it?"

Rostoff said smoothly, "I suggest, Bull, that in highest confidence we issue you one percent of the preferred stock of the Donal Mathers Radioactives Mining Corporation."

The other grunted contempt. "The word's already gone out that the dividends are going to be practically nothing. That you claim you're plowing back practically everything you take in, into the corporation."

Demming placed his fat hands over his fat belly and said, "That's the common stock, Bull. We're talking about the preferred. We've had to grease a few palms in Geneva, but the charter of this corporation is rather unique. In fact, as a result of Colonel Mathers' recommendations it comes under the head of Solar System Security and anyone wanting to make a thorough investigation of it would have his work cut out."

The labor leader grunted. "I see. I mighta known anything you two were connected with would have some fancy angles. One percent isn't enough. I'll need at least three."

"Three!" Rostoff blurted. "Are you drivel-happy, Frankle?"

Don Mathers was getting only about half of this. He hadn't known anything about a special charter that involved Solar System Security. He supposed that some of the endless papers he had signed without reading were involved.

Bull Frankle's expression was one of disgust. "At least three. Damn it, Max Rostoff, I'll have to spread it around but plenty, to keep my lieutenants in line. You don't think I run this by myself, do you? The One Big Union controls over a billion workers. You want to keep them quiet, don't you? No strikes, no slow-downs, no sit-downs, no nothing. Any trouble and my goons go in to quell it. I'm not just talking about the few tens of thousands on Mars and the satellites, though at the rate you're going there'll be shortly a damn sight more than that. I'm talking about all of your enterprises involved in this corporation to any extent whatsoever." He looked at Demming. "Take your Interplanetary Lines, for instance. Your maintenance men are muttering about a strike. Okay. I'll see there's no strike."

Rostoff and Demming looked at each other.

Rostoff said, "What do you say, Lawrence?"

Demming closed his eyes, but nodded.

Rostoff said, "It's a deal. Three percent."

The labor leader looked at Don suspiciously. "Don't he have a say?"

Rostoff said smoothly, "Colonel Mathers operates on other levels. He leaves business matters in our hands. That is, he can't be bothered with details."

Bull Frankle came to his feet after shooting Don a quick look of contempt. He said, "This is the biggest rip-off in history."

Rostoff nodded as near to pleasantly as his face allowed. "We've already come to that conclusion, Bull. And using practically the same words."

It was Si Mullens, Don's energetic public relations head, who came up with the brainstorm which was to become the beginning of the end for the space hero.

As the initial pressures of the forming of the corporation fell off and the speech load, interviews and so forth, lessened, Don needed new methods of keeping him in the public eyes to aid continuing common stock sales. At least, that was the way Demming and Rostoff saw it.

The autobiography had come out. Don hadn't known it was possible to write a book and get it into circulation so quickly. It was one of the biggest sellers of all time. And so far as Don was concerned, it was more fiction than biography. He recognized himself in the pages not at all, other than the illustrations. Where the ghost writer had obtained them all, he hadn't the slightest idea. There were photos, snapshots and otherwise, of all of his grandparents, his parents, and other more distant relatives, some of whom he had never known he had. All of them had seemingly led outstanding, productive and especially patriotic lives. He blinked when it turned out that his ancestors had been prominent in every major war ever fought by the United States, before the forming of the Solar System League. He blinked again to find that an ancestor had been Thomas Jefferson's right-hand aide when the Declaration of Independence was being written.

He was astonished to find how popular he had been from earliest childhood. How superlative he had been in school. How popular he had been in cadet school, at the Space Academy, and later among his squadron mates. It also turned out that for all practical purposes he didn't drink, had never smoked pot in his life, nor tobacco. As a matter of fact, the latter was true; one of the few true things in the thick book.

But back to Si Mullens, PR man supreme. He came up with the suggestion that Don make himself available for personal interview to anyone involved in the great project, the exploiting of the radioactives of the whole Solar System. Be they ever so humble, if they had a problem involving the Don Mathers Corporation they were free to consult him personally.

Most of them were unimportant. Most of them were largely desirous of meeting the great hero, of shaking his hand, of getting his signed photograph, or worshipping him a bit.

That was most of them. It took about a month for Dwight Schmidt to get in to see him.

Don went through the usual preliminaries, winding up with the old-timer sitting across from him, a soft drink in hand. The other was possibly in his mid-sixties and had obviously led life the hard way. He was only slightly stooped with long years of toil, still wiry, still strong, still fully alive and alert.

Don said, "What can I do for you, Mr. Schmidt?"

The only other person present was Dirck Bosch. Demming had given him the job of prompting Don, when Don was at sea which was often enough when dealing with the affairs of the corporation.

The old man said, "I'll lay it on the line, son, Don't

think I don't appreciate a man like you taking the trouble to listen to the problems of an old fart like me. But business is business, and survival is survival."

"That's what I'm here for, Mr. Schmidt."

"Mostly they call me Cobber. I was born in Australia, Colonel Mathers."

"Mostly they call me Don, Cobber," Don said.

"Fair dinkum. Now I don't want to take up much of your time. You must have less time than any man in Center City. This is how it is. I was one of the first pitchblende prospectors ever to work Callisto. And bad as it is now, it's nothing like it was in those days. I suppose I was first on Callisto before you was ever born, Don. Just a young joey, but hard working. To cut it short, I went into the outback there, put in some thirty Earth-years. When I ran out of money I got more from my parents, my relatives, my friends. They all believed in me. I worked like a dingo."

Don nodded. He glanced over at Bosch. Bosch, as usual, was expressionless.

The old-timer went on. "Finally, I hit it. Pretty rich. All of a sudden, me and all my friends was in business."

"Wonderful," Don said.

"Fair dinkum. Up until now. But when your new outfit—oh, I don't argue, I know we're all fighting the Kradens—but when your new outfit brought up my claims, they didn't pay as much for them as

we've put in down through the years. Not to speak
of my time, my whole life of searching. I wasn't left
with enough to pay off my debts, and these debts
were to relatives and my best friends."

Don shrunk back into himself. "Why'd you sell?
Why didn't you hold out for more?"

The old boy looked at him strangely. "Don't you
know the new laws? Senator Makowski pushed
them through. A man's *got* to sell. They're amalga-
mating every last ounce of uranium in the system.
They don't want any small operators, like me. For
efficiency, it's all got to be gathered together. The
better to fight the Kradens."

Don looked into Dirck Bosch's face, which remained expressionless.

He looked back at the aged prospector. "I . . . I
am afraid, uh, Cobber, this isn't something I know
about. All the evaluation of mines and so forth is
handled by experts. I don't even know them. I know
practically nothing about radioactives."

The other looked at him, puzzled. He said, "I
heard some of your talks over the Tri-Di, Don.
Sounds to me you understood pretty well."

Don said apologetically, "I've got a lot of experts,
speech writers, that sort of thing, who take care of
details."

"I see," the old man said wearily. He came to his
feet. "Then there's nothing you, personal, can do?"

Don said hurriedly, "I'll have my uh, secretary,

here take you to Mr. Rostoff, one of our, uh, special-ists. He's up on these things. Dirck, will you take Cobber to Mr. Rostoff?"

The Belgian raised his eyebrows and shrugged very slightly, but, "Certainly, Colonel Mathers," he said.

When the two had left, Don opened a desk drawer and brought forth a bottle of Demming's prehistoric brandy.

Very few persons think of themselves as bastards. The more perceptive, the more sensitive, the more vulnerable, might admit to occasional opportunism, may even commit acts which later they truly de-plore, in self-interest. But almost all of us can ex-plain almost all of the actions we take to our own satisfaction. It's the nature of the beasts that we are.

However, Don Mathers knocked back the slug of brandy with his now customary stiff-wristed motion.

He had been in space. The Almighty Ultimate knew he had been in space. He had even been on Callisto twice. Once had been more than enough. He couldn't understand how anyone, such as Dwight Schmidt, could spend the better part of his life there. No matter what the drive.

The next big one he took was possibly a month later.

He had been fielding them as best he could, spending two or three hours a day at it. He hated

Si Mullens and his brainstorm. Now there was no avoiding these people. He had to listen to them.

Sometimes, he wondered if he hadn't been better off as a One Man Scout pilot. And the hell with the Galactic Medal of Honor.

But no. There was no man on Earth who ate better than he did, drank better than he did, laid a more beautiful woman than he did. And, in the privacy of his own quarters, dressed better than he did. Expenses were meaningless. If he had wanted a half dozen Rembrandts he could have had them, if he had given a good goddamn about Rembrandts.

Besides, he was free of the Space Service and of the One Man Scouts. He was free of them. Demming and Rostoff had suggested that it might be well for him to take a trip to Callisto for publicity reasons, but for once he could tell them to stick it up their asses. He was never going to go into space again, short of being chained and dragged. Si Mullens could write all the press releases he wanted about Don's burning desire to get back into space, and he could stick such releases up his ass.

This time it was a committee, two elderly women and a middle-aged man. And all three looked anxious.

They went through the usual routine of introductions and Don taking their compliments and congratulations. Dirck Bosch got them seated and then took orders for one coffee and two soft drinks. They didn't particularly look as though they wanted the refreshments but who would turn down the opportunity to be able to say later that they'd had a drink with the bearer of the Galactic Medal of Honor?

When all were settled down, Don smiled encouragingly and said, "And now what can I do for you?"

They looked from one to the other and evidently decided to let the man become the spokesman.

He put down his coffee and said, "We're stockholders, or were, in Callisto Pitchblende, Incorporated."

Don nodded. He had never heard of the outfit.

The man said, "I don't know if you know about the early days of the company. It started more or less from scratch, compared to most interplanetary businesses. On a shoestring, so to speak. It was largely financed by a good many people who didn't have a great deal to invest. But the promised dividends made it look like a good investment and it turned out to be just that." He hesitated.

Don nodded encouragingly but inwardly he knew what was coming and this was going to be one of the bad ones.

The other went on doggedly. "A lot of us stockholders had put everything we had into Callisto Pitchblende, life savings, that sort of thing. Most of us depended on the dividends to live. Some of us had no other income at all. Most of us, perhaps. Well, at any rate, when your corporation took us over, it issued one common share of your Radioactives Mining Corporation for each share of our company. And we're just as patriotic as anyone else. Nobody complained. But then, last month, it came out that your corporation was going to pay only a three percent dividend."

One of the women said, desperation in her voice, "That's not enough to keep up with inflation. The way inflation is going, in five years my shares of stock won't be worth the paper."

The other woman said, "And now with the new laws, we can't even sell our shares."

Don frowned at her. "How do you mean?"

Dirck Bosch cleared his throat, "Colonel Mathers, the new law pertaining to the corporation. For at least ten years, anyone owning shares cannot sell them."

Don looked at him blankly.

The committee waited.

Don said finally, "This is not my particular field. I'll turn you over to one of my associates. Dirck, will you take these ladies and gentleman to Mr. Rostoff's office?" He stood to see them to the door.

Behind their backs, Dirck Bosch shook his head in resignation, but escorted the others, who paused long enough to shake hands with Don once again. They shook quite enthusiastically.

When they were gone, Don Mathers got out his bottle of cognac. He took a hefty slug from it, then reached over and picked up a half full glass of the soft drink Bosch had brought one of the women and used it for a chaser.

He was sitting there, breathing deeply, the bottle still on his desk, when Maximilian Rostoff came bursting in, shortly after followed by the Belgian secretary.

Rostoff, his face livid, ripped out, "What's the idea of pushing off these stupid marks on me? What do you think we gave you the job for? I can't waste my time cooling indignant suckers."

Don flushed angrily. "Look," he said. "Don't push me too far. You need me. Plenty. In fact, from what I can see, this corporation needs me more than it does you." He was scornful. "Originally, the idea was that you put up the money. What money? All the pseudo-dollar credit needed is coming from sale of nearly worthless common stock. You were also to put up the brains. What brains? We've hired the best mining engineers, the best technicians, the best scientists, to do their end, the best corporation executives to do that end. You and Demming aren't needed."

Max Rostoff's face had grown wolfishly thin in his anger. He took in the open bottle on the desk. "Look, bottle-baby," he sneered, "you're the only one who's vulnerable in this set-up. There's not a single thing that Demming and I can be held accountable for. You have no beefs coming, for that matter. You're getting everything you ever wanted. You've got a swanky place to live in. You eat the best food in the solar system. And, most important of all to a rummy, you drink the best guzzle and as much of it as you want. What's more, unless either Demming or I go to the bother, you'll never be exposed. You'll live your life out being the biggest hero in the system."

It was Don Mathers' turn to sneer. "What do you mean, I'm the only one vulnerable? There's no evidence against me, Rostoff, and you know it. Who'd listen to you if you sounded off? I burned that Kraden cruiser until there wasn't a sign to be found that would indicate it wasn't operational when I first spotted it."

Rostoff snorted amusement, or as near to amusement as he was capable of. He said, "Don't be an ass, Mathers. We took a series of photos of that derelict when we stumbled on it. Not only can we prove that you didn't knock it out, we can prove that it was in good shape before you worked it over. I even took some shots in the interior. I imagine that Space Fleet technicians would have loved to have seen the inner workings of that Kraden cruiser—before you loused it up."

"If you opened up on me, you'd be revealed too."

"No, we wouldn't," Rostoff laughed. "We could announce that we'd been just about ready to reveal the presence of the derelict when we were flabbergasted to find that you claimed to have destroyed it. We hardly knew what to do when you received the decoration. We were afraid of disrupting solar system morale."

Don was speechless.

Rostoff chuckled flatly. "I wonder what kind of a court-martial they give to an interplanetary hero who turns out to be a saboteur."

XVII

After Rostoff had left, slamming the door behind him, Don grabbed up the bottle of cognac and took a deep swig. Then he slapped it down to the desk again and glared at Dirck Bosch.

Bosch shook his head, his face, as usual, expressionless. "The bottle is no answer," he said.

"How the hell would you know, you plastic doll?"

"Tried it."

"What is the answer?"

The Belgian shook his head. "I don't know. They are more ruthless men than we are . . . Don." It was the first time he had ever called Don Mathers by his first name. "Men who are completely, completely, ruthless can sweep all before them. Rostoff, and especially Demming, are probably the most ruthless men in the solar system."

Don took up the bottle again. He said, "Like a drink, Dirck?"

The other shook his head. "No. Like I said, I tried that route. I don't suppose you'll be wanting to interview any more today."

"No," Don said.

Dirck Bosch left. To cancel any more of the day's appointments, Don assumed.

He took up the bottle and took one more belt from it then threw it against the wall. Screw Lawrence Demming's million dollar guzzle.

He went over to the room's elevator door and flung it open. Inside, was one of the always present bodyguards.

Don said, "Get the hell out."

The guard, whose name escaped Don, there were so damned many of them around the place, said, apologetically, "Colonel, my orders are——"

"You can stick your orders up your rosy-red rectum," Don told him in the language of his cadet days. "Get out of there."

The guard got.

Don said to the order screen, "Motor pool, in the basement."

"Yes, sir," the screen said. "Colonel Mathers, our orders are——"

"Screw your orders."

That command stopped the metallic computer voice only a moment. He had never heard a phone screen hum before. This one hummed only for the briefest of moments and then said, "The motor pool. Yes, Colonel Mathers."

In the motor pool, he summoned an automated hovercab. While he waited, several persons approached him, as usual. He snarled at them. When the cab came he got in and dialed the entertainment area of Center City.

He began the biggest, most prolonged toot of his life, and in his time Donal Mathers had been on some king-sized binges.

From time to time the fog would roll in on him and when it would roll out again he couldn't remember where he was, how he had gotten there, or what had been happening just previously. Usually, he found himself in some sort of nightclub or bar. He would immediately order again and take up where he left off. He assumed that he was still in Center City but he couldn't be sure. Hell, he might be in SanSan, London or Bombay.

It was when he came out of one of these alcoholic dazes that he found her seated across the table from him. They were in some sort of night spot. He didn't recognize it.

He licked his lips and scowled at the taste of stale vomit. He slurred, "Hello, Di. Cheers, cheers. What spins?"

Dian Keramikou said, "Hi, Don."

He said, "I thought you were on Callisto."

She laughed at him. "We went through all that. I've been back over a month. It seems that the gravity on Callisto didn't agree with me. It's only slightly larger than Luna and with a gravity only two tenths that of Earth. I was continually nauseated. Finally, they shipped me home. This is the third time I've told you about it."

He said, "I must've blanked out. Guess I've been hitting it a little hard."

She laughed again. "You mean you don't remember all the things you've been telling me the past two hours?" She was obviously quite sober. Dian had never been much for the guzzle.

Don looked at her narrowly. "What've I been telling you for the past two hours?"

"Mostly about how it was when you were a little boy. About fishing and your first .22 rifle. And the time you shot the squirrel and then felt so sorry."

"Oh," Don said. He ran his right hand over his mouth.

There was an ice bucket beside him, but the bottle of ersatz champagne in it was empty. He looked about the room for a waiter. People at nearby tables would shoot looks at him from time to time, but none approached. He got the feeling that possibly some of them had tried earlier and that he had run them off, probably nastily.

Dian said gently, "Do you really think you need any more, Don?"

He looked across the table at her. She was as beautiful as ever. Not a glamour type like Alicia but for Donal Mathers the most beautiful woman in the world.

Don said, "Look, I can't remember. Did we get married, or something?"

Her laugh trilled. "Married! I only ran into you two or three hours ago." She hesitated before saying further, "I had assumed you were deliberately avoiding me. Center City isn't as big as all that."

Don Mathers said shakily, "Well, if we're not married, let me decide when I want another bottle of the grape."

Dian flushed. "Sorry, Don."

The headwaiter approached, bearing another magnum of the ersatz champagne. He bobbed at Don Mathers. "Having a good time, Colonel?"

"Okay," Don said shortly. When the other was gone he downed a full glass and felt the fumes almost immediately.

He said to Dian, "I haven't been avoiding you. We haven't met is all. I don't get out much—being a celebrity is a hazard—and didn't know you were back on Earth. But even if I had known, I don't know whether or not I'd have looked you up." He twisted the knife in his own wound. "The way I remember it, the last time we saw each other, you gave me quite a slap in the face. The way I remember, you didn't think I was hero enough for you." He poured another glass of the wine, hating himself.

Dian's face was still flushed. She said, her voice very low, "I misunderstood you, Don. Even after your defeat of that Kraden cruiser, I still, I admit, think I basically misunderstood you. I told myself that it could have been done by any pilot of a One Man Scout, given that one in a million break. It just happened to be you, who made that suicide dive attack that succeeded. A thousand other pilots might have also taken the million-to-one suicide chance rather than let the Kraden escape."

"Yeah," Don said. Even in his alcohol, he was surprised at her words. He said gruffly, "Sure, anybody might have done it. A pure fluke. But why'd you change your mind about me? How come the switch of heart?"

"Because of what you've done since, darling."

He closed one eye, the better to focus. "Since?"

He recognized the expression in her dark eyes. A touch of star gleam. That little girl receptionist when he had gone to the Interplanetary Lines Building, on his return from Geneva. The honeymooner in Geneva. Even Alicia. In fact, in the past few months Don had seen it in many feminine eyes. And all for him.

Dian said, "Instead of cashing in on your fame, you've devoted yourself, unselfishly, to something even more important to the defense than bringing down individual Kraden cruisers."

Don looked at her. He could feel a nervous tic beginning in his left eyebrow. Finally, he reached for the champagne bottle again and refilled his glass. He said, "You really go for this hero stuff, don't you?"

She said nothing, but the starshine was still in her eyes.

He made his voice deliberately sour. "Look, suppose I asked you to come back to my place tonight?"

"Yes," she said, so softly as hardly to be heard.

"And told you to bring your overnight bag along," he added brutally.

Dian Keramikou looked into his face. "Why are you twisting yourself, your inner-self, so hard, Don? Of course I'd come, if that's what you wanted."

"And then," he said flatly, "suppose I kicked you out in the morning?"

Dian winced, but kept her eyes even with his, her own moist now. "You forget," she whispered. "You have been awarded the Galactic Medal of Honor, the bearer of which can do no wrong."

"Almighty Ultimate!" Don muttered in soul defeat. He filled his glass, still once again, motioning to a nearby captain of waiters who was obviously hovering only for his orders.

"Yes, Colonel," the captain said.

Don said, "Look, in about five minutes I'm going to pass out. See that I get to some hotel, any hotel, will you? And that this young lady gets to her apartment. And, waiter, just send my bill to the Radioactives Mining Corporation."

The other bowed. "The manager's instructions, sir, are that Colonel Mathers must never see a bill in this establishment."

Dian said, worrying over the new drink he was taking, "Don!"

He didn't look at her. He raised his glass to his mouth and shortly afterward the fog rolled in again.

When it rolled out, the unfamiliar taste of black

coffee was in his mouth. He shook his head in an attempt to achieve clarity.

He seemed to be in some working class type auto-cafeteria. Next to him, in a booth, was a fresh faced sub-lieutenant of the—Don squinted at the collar tabs—yes, of the Space Service. A One Man Scout pilot.

Don stuttered, "Cheers. What spins?"

The pilot said apologetically, "Sub-lieutenant Pierpont, sir. You seemed so far under the weather that I thought I'd best take over. No disrespect, sir."

"Oh, you did, eh?"

"Well, yes sir. You were, well, reclining in the gutter, sir. In spite of your, well, appearance, your condition, I recognized you, sir."

"Oh," Don got out. His stomach was an objecting turmoil.

The lieutenant said, "Want to try some more of this coffee now, sir? Or maybe some soup or a sandwich?"

Don groaned, "No, no thanks. I don't think I could hold it down."

The pilot grinned. "You must have thrown a classic, Colonel Mathers."

"I guess so. Don't call me Colonel. I'm a damned civilian now. What time is it? No, that doesn't make any difference. What's the date?"

Pierpont told him and then added, "You'll always be Colonel Mathers to me, sir. I have your photograph above my bed, and in the cockpit of my Scout."

The date was hard to believe. The last he could remember, he had been with Di. With Dian in some nightclub. He wondered how long ago that had been.

He growled at the lieutenant, "Well, how go the One Man Scouts?"

Pierpont grinned back at him. "Glad to be out of them, sir?"

"Usually."

Pierpont looked at him strangely. He said, "I don't blame you, sir. But it isn't as bad as it used to be when you were still in the Space Service, Colonel."

Don grunted at that opinion. He said, "How come? Two weeks to a month, all by yourself, watching the symptoms of space cafard progress. Then three weeks of leave to get drunk in, get laid in, and then another stretch in deep space."

The pilot snorted in deprecation. "That's the way it used to be," he said. He fingered the spoon in his coffee cup. "That's the way it still should be, of course. But it isn't. They're spreading the duty around now and I spend less than one week out of four on patrol."

Don hadn't been listening too closely, but now he looked up. "What'd ya mean?"

Pierpont said, "I mean, sir—I suppose this isn't bridging security, seeing who you are, but fuel stocks are running so low, in spite of all *your* efforts, that we can't maintain full patrols any more, especially of the Monitors and the other larger spacecraft."

There was a cold emptiness in Don Mathers' stomach.

He said, "Look, I'm still woozy. Say that again, Lieutenant."

The lieutenant told him again.

Don Mathers rubbed the back of his hand over his mouth and tried to think.

He said, finally, "Look, Lieutenant, first let's get another cup of coffee into me and maybe that sandwich you were talking about. And then would you help me to get back to my place?"

He might be drunk, and he might not be up on the inner workings of the Donal Mathers Radioactives Corporation, but he knew damn well that production of uranium had zoomed since its founding.

XVIII

It took him four days, even with the aid of Anti-Alc and some Vitamin B-Complex shots. During that period, he kept in seclusion, not even seeing Alicia.

And during the four days, something that Eric Hansen had said to him came back, and with it some of the things Thor Bjornsen had said.

When he had gotten to the point where his hands no longer trembled, he cleaned himself up thoroughly, ate a good breakfast, dressed carefully, then went into his study. He sat down at the desk and looked into the library booster screen. He dialed the Interplanetary Data Banks and then Information.

A sharp-looking young man's face faded in and Don said, "Run off all the video-tapes that were taken of the battle between the Kradens and the four Earth fleets, fifty years ago."

The young man widened his eyes. He said, "Just a moment, sir."

His face faded to be replaced shortly by an older man's. This one wore the uniform of a space admiral.

He said, "Colonel Mathers! What a pleasure to speak to you."

Don said, "Great. I want to see all of the video-tapes taken of the battle between the Kradens and the Earth fleets, half a century ago."

The other frowned. He said, carefully, "Well, actually, Colonel, we have an edited version, which runs for approximately one hour, that is for public consumption. I imagine you saw it as a cadet at the Space Academy."

"Yes, I did," Don said impatiently. "That's not what I want. I want the complete unedited tapes, every one taken."

"I assure you, Colonel Mathers, due to the pressures and excitement at the time, those video-tapes were photographed in most haphazard and slipshod fashion. Literally scores of different cameras were trained on the fight at one time or the other." He gave a small laugh. "Later, some were to find that they had forgotten to put tapes in the cameras. Others found . . . Well, at any rate, Colonel, they're a hodgepodge. I'm glad I didn't have the job of editing them into the coherent story."

Don said, "Nevertheless, I want to see them all."

The fleet admiral stared at him for a long moment. Finally, he said, "I am most sorry, Colonel, but some of the video-tapes are restricted, for security reasons."

Don said, "I am Donal Mathers, as you well know, and I wish to see those video-tapes. Are you

263

suggesting that I am not cleared for highest security? If you do not begin screening those video-tapes for me immediately, I shall get in touch with President Kwame Kumasi of the Solar System League and we will soon find if there is anything in the Interplanetary Data Banks so restricted that a holder of the Galactic Medal of Honor can't see it. I shall further suggest to the President and to the media that in my estimation you are incompetent."

The fleet admiral gave up, his face resigned. "Very well, Colonel. However, I have one request. When you are through, please call me again. I will wish to discuss them with you."

Don leaned back in his chair. "The video-tapes, please. All of them."

Within moments, they began flashing on the screen. There were hours upon hours of them. Evidently, all four of the Earth space fleets had taken tape after tape. The space admiral had been correct, many of them, probably most of them, were a mess. Some consisted of nothing whatsoever save shots of empty space.

But some. . . .

Thor Bjornsen was right. It had been a balls-up.

The four Earth fleets, those of the United States, Common Europe, the Soviet Complex and China, had zeroed-in like madmen, all firing everything they had, missiles, laser beams, flakflak guns of all categories, firing wildly.

There was no sign he could make out of the Kra-

dens firing back, although, of course, there was always some chance of them using weapons that were
undetectable with Earth equipment.

Don flinched when he saw a Common Europe
cruiser misdirect a laser beam and cut entirely
through a Chinese cruiser, and winced again when
two American Two Man Scouts crashed headlong
into each other.

The Kradens, seemingly completely confused at
this hysterical attack, broke their original neat
formation, at first sped up unbelievingly, and then
disappeared, leaving only the smoldering hulks of
their destroyed craft behind.

But the hysterical shooting, beaming and launch-
ing of nuclear missiles continued on for possibly an
hour more. Spacecraft of the four fleets darted
about, firing, sometimes colliding.

It was the most horrifying spectacle Don Mathers
had ever witnessed, and the most senseless. Thor
Bjornsen had been right. Those so-called Kradens
had not been a military expedition. What they had
been, only the Almighty Ultimate knew. Merchants
or ambassadors attempting to contact other intelligent life forms? Who could know?

And then another truth came home to him. That
Kraden derelict which he had beamed over and over
with his flakflak gun. It hadn't been a new arrival.
Not even, as Thor had tried to figure out, a new
missionary to attempt to establish contact with the
aggressive human race. It had been a leftover from

the first conflict. It had been destroyed in the first contact and had been drifting in space for half a century, undetected. He didn't know, but possibly the Kradens had devices, still operative over all the decades, that could repulse Earth type sensors. Or possibly their crafts were made of some material that radar wouldn't pick up.

When it was all over, he flicked off the screen and sank back into his chair. All his instincts were to go to the auto-bar and dial himself a bottle; but he didn't. He had to think.

He attempted to recapitulate and it came hard. It was all too unbelievable.

There had been a cover-up. There must have been. The greatest cover-up of all history. The biggest military lie of all time. Bigger than the reports Cortes and his men had made of the conquest of Mexico.

It came to him how it could have been done. Most of those involved in the fight had no complete picture of what was happening. Four Earth fleets were in the hysterical mess. There was no central command, largely they couldn't even understand each other's languages. They simply lit in, each spacecraft, each man, for himself. Chaos!

And then when it was all over, they returned triumphantly to Earth, now united, now no longer four space fleets, but one. Then the highest ranking officers had compiled the mass of video-tapes that had been taken, combined them. *And then they must have known*. Then they must have realized. And, like the military down through the ages, they covered-up. They and the industrial-military complex behind them.

Those at the top could not afford to admit they had attacked, without provocation, a peaceful armada from outer space. They couldn't afford to lose their high positions, their prestige, their commands.

Those who had raised voices of dissent, assuming there were any, must have been suppressed. The military-industrial apparatus must have swung into high gear. Why, otherwise, were these video-tapes supposedly of high security nature? Security against whom? The Kradens? Obviously, the Kradens couldn't possibly have access to them. The security applied only to Earthlings, members of the human race. They were the ones from whom the information was being withheld.

And why?

He reactivated the library booster screen, dialed, and said, "I wish to know what corporations are most active in trying to breakthrough in the field of nuclear fusion."

It was the same sharp looking young man that he had confronted hours earlier.

He said, "That information is restricted, Colonel."

"I know, I know," Don said wearily. "However —"

"Yes, Colonel Mathers."

It took some digging around, but it finally

emerged that Lawrence Demming and Maximilian Rostoff dominated the various organizations that were working on nuclear fusion, none of which, for various reasons, were having much luck. Scientists died, sometimes under strange circumstances; projects, seemingly doing fine, were aborted; this, that and the other thing. Seemingly the project was jinxed.

It didn't take much to come to the conclusion that Demming and Rostoff didn't want nuclear fusion to take over from the uranium utilizing nuclear fission.

So he finally stood and made his way to the elevator and instructed it to take him to the reception room of Demming's private sanctum sanctorum, where the other usually was at this time of day.

At the entrance to the inner sanctum was posted one of the bodyguards.

Don said, "I want to see Demming."

The bodyguard said, politely enough, "You don't have an appointment, Colonel Mathers, and he and Mr. Rostoff are having a conference. He says to keep everybody out."

"That doesn't apply to me," Don snapped. "Get out of my way."

The other barred the way, saying reluctantly, "He said it applied to everybody, Colonel Mathers."

Don put his full weight into a blow that started at his waist, dug deep into the other's middle. The guard doubled forward, his eyes bugging. Don gripped his hands together into a double fist and brought them upward in a vicious uppercut.

The other fell forward and to the floor.

Don stood over him for a moment, watchful for movement which didn't develop. The hefty bodyguard wasn't as tough as he looked. Had he moved, Don would have kicked him in the side of the head.

He knelt and fished from under the other's left arm a vicious looking short-barreled laser pistol. He tucked it under his own jacket into his belt, then turned and opened the door and entered the supposedly barred office.

Demming and Rostoff looked up from their work across a double desk. The subservient Dirck Bosch was, as usual, on his feet and in the background a bit. Somewhat to Don's surprise, Alicia was also present, seated to one side, rather idly going through an old-fashioned hardcover book.

She said, "Why, Don. Where have you been this last week or so?"

"Learning the facts of life," he told her.

Demming leaned back in his swivel chair and said, "You're sober for a change."

Don Mathers pulled up a stenographer's chair and straddled it, leaning his arms on the back. He said coldly, "Comes a point when even the lowest worm turns. I've been checking out a few things."

Demming grunted amusement.

Don said, "Space patrols have been cut far back, although the people haven't been informed of the fact."

Rostoff snorted. "Is that supposed to interest us? That's the problem of the military and the government."

"Oh, it interests us, all right," Don growled. "Currently, the corporation controls probably five-sixths of the system's uranium."

Demming said in greasy satisfaction, "More like seven-eights and increasing by the week."

"Why, then?" Don said bluntly. "Why are you doing what you're doing?"

They both scowled but another element was present in their expressions too. They thought the question unintelligent. Alicia put down her book and frowned puzzlement.

Demming closed his eyes and said in his porcine manner, "Tell him, Max."

Rostoff said, "Look, Mathers, don't be stupid. Remember when we told you, during that first interview, that we wanted your name in the corporation, among other reasons, because we could use a man who was above the law? That a maze of ridiculous binding ordinances have been laid on business through the centuries?"

"I remember," Don said bitterly.

"Well, it goes both ways. Government today is also bound, very strongly, and even in great emergency, not to interfere in business. These complicated laws balance each other, you might say. Our whole legal system is based on them. Right now, we've got government right where we want it. This is free enterprise, Mathers, at its pinnacle. Did you ever read about Jim Fisk and his attempt to corner gold in 1869, the so-called Black Friday affair? Well, Jim Fisk was a peanut peddler compared to us."

"What's this got to do with the Space Fleet having insufficient fuel to. . . ." Don Mathers stopped as comprehension came to him. "You're holding our radioactives off the market, pressuring the government for a price rise which it can't afford."

Demming opened his eyes and said fatly, "For triple the old price, Mathers. Before we're through, we'll corner half the wealth in the system."

Don looked at him in disgust. "And supposedly we're fighting a war. But that isn't all I've hit on gentlemen. I've also come to the conclusion that it's you two who are sabotaging the nuclear fusion project. How many times has nuclear fusion been discovered in the past couple of decades?"

Rostoff smiled wolfishly. "Three times."

"And all three times you suppressed it?"

"That's right. You wouldn't expect us to destroy our markets for uranium, would you, Mathers? Nuclear fusion would make power practically free."

Don was shaking his head. "But even that isn't all. The fact of the matter is, there is no war."

Alicia said, her frown deeper, "What are you saying?"

He didn't bother to look at her. "There is no war, because there are no Kradens, and haven't been since fifty years ago. They appeared for a very short period, discovered that we were hostile, and disappeared, never to return. Well, I'm blowing the whistle, gentlemen."

Alicia was beautiful but far from dumb. She said, "Don! Don't be ridiculous. If you do anything foolish, it will mean the collapse of father's empire. Why, we could become penniless overnight! There wouldn't be anything left for me to inherit."

He didn't answer her.

Lawrence Demming said, "Leave the room, Alicia. We'll handle this madman."

She got up, gave Don one last pitying look, and followed her father's instructions.

When she was gone, Demming said, "Take him, Dirck."

But the Belgian shook his head. "No," he said. "This worm, too, has turned, Demming. I don't care what happens to me, or my family—stopping you is the only important thing. Over the years, I've learned a great deal of the business of the Demming and Rostoff corporations. I have no particular desire to live. But I'll continue to do so, at least until I've helped Don with my testimony."

Surprisingly fast for such a fat man, Lawrence Demming's hand flitted into a desk drawer to emerge with a twin of the laser pistol tucked into Don's belt.

Don Mathers grinned at him calmly, even as he pushed his jacket back to reveal the butt of his own weapon. He made no attempt to draw it however.

He said softly, "Shoot me, Demming, and you've killed the most popular man in the Solar System. There'd be no place to hide, no matter how much money you have; the whole human race would be seeking you out. On the other hand, if I should kill you. . . ."

He put his left hand into his pocket and it emerged with a small, ordinary bit of red ribbon on which was suspended a platinum cross. He displayed it on his palm.

The fat man's face whitened at the ramifications and his hand relaxed to let the gun drop to the desk top.

"Liston, Donal," he broke out. "We've been unrealistic with you. We'll reverse ourselves and split, honestly—split three ways."

Don Mathers laughed at him. "Trying to bribe me with money, Demming? Why, don't you realize that I'm the only man in existence who has no use for money, who can't spend money? That my fellow men, whom I've done such a good job of betraying, have honored me to a point where money is meaningless?"

Max Rostoff snatched up the fallen gun, snarling, "I'm calling your bluff, you gutless rummy. And when I've finished you, I'll deal with Bosch."

Don Mathers said, "Okay, Rostoff. There's just

two other things I want to say first. One, like Dirck, here, I don't care if I live or not. I've destroyed too much of what was decent, to care if I live or not. Two—you're only fifteen feet or so away, but you know what I think? I think you're probably a lousy shot. I don't think you've had much practice. I think I can get my gun out and cut you down before you can finish me." He grinned thinly. "Wanta try?"

Max Rostoff snarled a curse and his finger whitened on the trigger.

Don Mathers fell sideward to the floor and rolled, his hand streaking for his weapon. Without thought, there came back to him the hours of training as a cadet in hand weapons, in judo, in hand to hand combat. Anachronistic the training might have been, but they gave it to you. He went into action with cool confidence.

AFTERMATH

From the Geneva Spaceport he took an automated hovercab to the Presidential Palace. At the palace gates he found he had left his credit card back in Center City. He snorted wearily. It was the first time in months that he'd had to pay for anything.

Four sentries were standing at attention. He said, "Do one of you boys have a Universal Credit Card to pay off this cab? I seem to have mislaid mine."

A sergeant grinned, approached and did the necessary.

Don said, "I don't know how you go about this. I don't have an appointment, but I want to see the president."

"We can turn you over to one of his aides, Colonel Mathers," the sergeant said. "We can't go any further than that. While we're waiting, what's the chance of getting your autograph, sir? I gotta kid. . . ."

Don sighed, then took a deep breath and said, "He'll probably tear it up before the week's out."

"No sir, Colonel. He'll treasure it the rest of his life."

It wasn't nearly as complicated as Don thought it would be. In less than half an hour he was seated in the president's office. How long had it been since this man had given him his decoration? Could it be less than a year?

He told the story completely, making no effort to spare himself. At the end, he stood up long enough to put a paper in front of the other, then sat down again.

He said, "I'm turning the whole corporation over to the government. . . ."

President Kwame Kumasi, whose ebony face had been registering shock after shock, the past hour, said, "Just a moment, Colonel Mathers. My administration does not advocate State ownership of industry."

"I know. When the State controls industry you only put the whole mess off one step. The question then becomes, who controls the State? However, I'm not arguing political economy with you, Mr. President. You didn't let me finish. I'm turning it over to the government to untangle, even while making use of the radioactives. There's going to be a lot of untangling to do. Demming and Rostoff were devious and complicated, to say the least. So are some of the others they brought into the, ah, action. Reimbursing the prospectors and small operators who were blackjacked out of their holdings; reimbursing the miners and other laborers who were squeezed into accepting minimal pay in the name of patriotism." Don Mathers shrugged unhappily. "On top of everything else, for all these people victimized, the uranium will be all but useless once it is learned that there have been nuclear fusion breakthroughs."

"Yes," the president said. He sighed deeply. "And you say that Maximilian Rostoff is dead?"

"Yes, I killed him. And Demming has gone completely drivel-happy. I think he was always a little unbalanced and the prospect of losing all that money, the greatest fortune ever conceived of, tipped the scales."

President Kumasi said, "And what about you, Colonel Mathers?"

Don took a deep breath. "I suppose that after my court-martial, or civilian trial, or whatever, I'll ——"

The president interrupted gently, "You seem to forget, Colonel Mathers. You carry the Galactic Medal of Honor, the bearer of which can do no wrong."

Don Mathers gaped at him.

The president smiled, albeit a bit sourly. "It would hardly do for human morale, in this period which will shake our concepts, to find that our supreme symbol of heroism was a phoney. Colonel, there will be no trial and you will retain your decoration."

Don was still gaping. "But it will have to come out that the Kraden cruiser I supposedly destroyed was already a derelict. Otherwise, no one will believe that the Kradens were not hostile. Otherwise, everyone will believe that they came back again. Otherwise, all our people will believe that the so-called war must go on."

The president shook his head. "I think I have that figured out. At the same time that we announce that the original battle was a terrible mistake, and that the Kradens were a peaceful fleet of spaceships, we will announce that our technicians, examining the Miro Class cruiser which you destroyed, found it unarmed and obviously a spaceship sent to attempt to reopen negotiations with us, in spite of our initial attack upon them fifty years earlier. No blame will be placed on you, who, in good faith, went in to the attack, believing that you were fighting an enemy. It was all a great mistake, but your courage and gallantry were still there. You deserved the award, in spite of the tragedy. Meanwhile, we shall immediately put our tight laser beams on Luna to working trying to contact the Kradens—wherever in space they may be located—and utilizing the most recently developed methods of attempting to communicate with extraterrestrials—to apologize for our mistake and to reopen contact with them."

"You mean, I am to retain my medal?"

"Yes, the human race would be hard put to bear the psychic upset if you were to be stripped of it."

"But, I don't want it!"

The president rubbed a weary black hand over his short, kinky hair. "I am afraid that is the cross you will have to bear the rest of your life, Colonel Mathers. I do not suppose it will be an easy one." His eyes went to a far corner of the room, but unseeingly. He said, after a long moment, "However, I am not so very sure about you not deserving your award, Colonel."